IN THE BAG

ALISSA GROSSO

GLITTER
PIGEON
PRESS

SATURDAY

I

SIXTEEN YEARS AGO, Tamsyn was thrust into parent-hood without an instruction manual, and she felt like she had been making things up as she went along ever since. She wished she had that missing instruction manual as she stood outside her son's locked bedroom door, trying to rouse Sean from his deep slumber. When had he started locking his door? Should she say something to him about this? She understood that he needed his privacy, but how much privacy was too much?

Each year the township organized a spring clean-up day. Each year she and Sean dutifully donned their neon yellow safety vests, ate the free donuts the Jaycees provided and helped to clean up roadside litter. It was their thing, a sort of mother-son tradition. Not as fun as say, picking apples in the fall, but even in the trash clean-up they found fun.

They marveled together at what pigs people could be, dumping all their detritus at the side of the road. They found humor in the weird randomness of the things they discovered, like the toupee, the shopping bag filled with fake fruit and a terrible love poem that had been written to someone named Madeline. Once Tamsyn had found a five-dollar bill, and a few years ago Sean had been ridiculously excited to discover some rare Pokémon card.

She had been reminding him about the clean-up for the past several days. Not in subtle ways, either, because she had learned that her teenage son was not too swift at picking up on subtleties. So the fact that her knock on his locked door earned nothing more than a grunt from him annoyed her.

"Woman, just let him sleep," Ken said as he shuffled down the hallway.

Her husband had still been asleep when she'd gotten out of bed, but apparently the noise she was making in the hallway must have woke him.

From within Sean's room, she heard a rustle. He was awake at least.

Tamsyn seized on this opportunity. "Sean, we're going to be late."

"Not going," Sean said.

"Are you feeling sick?" Tamsyn asked.

"Just let him sleep already," Ken said.

"We're supposed to go do the clean-up today," Tamsyn said.

"Just because you want to go be a slave and clean up other people's trash doesn't mean he has to," Ken said.

"I've got homework to do," Sean said.

"He's old enough to make his own decisions," Ken added.

Tamsyn realized Ken was probably right. When she was just a few years older than Sean was now, she'd become a mother. She had to stop treating Sean like he was a child, but he seemed so much younger and less mature than she had been at that age. Or maybe that's just the way it seemed to her, looking back on things.

Still, she felt it was important to instill a sense of responsibility. Showing him how to be a productive and contributing member of society seemed like an important thing. Not that Ken understood that.

Well, she was the one who wanted Sean to have a father around, a male influence, and that was Ken, so maybe she needed to listen to him.

She was still on the fence about things when she got behind the wheel of her car a few minutes later. She sat in the driveway, staring at the house as if she could will Sean to change his mind, but she knew that wasn't going to happen.

2

Gravel crunched under Tamsyn's tires as she pulled into the unpaved parking lot adjacent to the municipal park. She spotted Marlena's RAV4, with its proud-parent-of-an-honor-student bumper sticker, and parked next to it. A light layer of fog hung over the meeting area for the clean-up. Volunteers in neon vests headed out with trash bags in their hands to go clean up litter. And there, standing by the table waiting for her, was Marlena and her son Philip. Tamsyn didn't know a thing about Philip's absent father. Obviously he had been black, and judging by the way Marlena still towered over her thin son, Tamsyn assumed he too had been small and slim. What she did know was that Philip seemed to be doing more or less okay without a dad around. Moreover, Philip was here today, and Sean wasn't.

Tamsyn was late. She hated to be late, but the incident with Sean this morning had set her back a few minutes. She quickly grabbed her fleece jacket form the backseat, pulled it on and zipped it up. She stepped out of the car and walked across the dew-soaked grass to where Marlena and Philip were waiting.

Philip was almost the same age as Sean, less than a year younger. Eleven years ago, when Tamsyn had started working at the social security office, she had been excited to learn that her coworker had a son Sean's age. She'd imagined them becoming good friends. She'd pictured the four of them--she and Marlena, Sean and Philip, going on outings together and hanging out. But Sean and Philip had never really hit it off. They weren't enemies, but they moved in different circles. Philip was serious, studious, a bit of a book nerd. And then there was Sean. What was Sean exactly? He liked his video games. He spent hours in his room playing them, hanging out on the internet forums. It was a world that Tamsyn was only dimly aware of, and the truth was, she wasn't really sure what made her son tick.

"I was starting to think you weren't going to make it," Marlena said. "Sean's not with you?"

"He wasn't feeling well this morning," Tamsyn said. She felt bad lying, but at the same time she felt like Marlena's remark was some sort of dig at her parenting or at Sean.

"He's got a case of Ken-itis maybe," Marlena said.

Marlena had never liked Ken, and that was before Tamsyn had confided in her.

Philip stood beside Marlena, leaning against the folding table that held boxes of industrial trash bags, his eyes glued to his phone. That's how these kids were today, always on their phones. In that way, he was exactly like Sean.

"I got you a vest," Marlena said. Marlena's bracelet sparkled in the light as she handed the neon safety vest to Tamsyn. The bracelet was too fancy for cleaning up trash, but Marlena never took the thing off. It was one of those Pandora charm bracelets, and she never passed up an opportunity to tell people about the significance of the different charms and the perfect son who had purchased them for her. The last Christmas gift Sean had given Tamsyn was a pair of slipper socks.

"Ken's not the reason Sean couldn't make it," Tamsyn said, and she didn't know why she felt the need to protect her husband this morning. It wasn't maybe a complete lie. Sean hadn't been about to come even before Ken intervened.

"I'm just saying, I don't see him here," Marlena said. "Come to think of it, I never have."

Marlena didn't like to pass up an opportunity to remind Tamsyn that she was a fool for not leaving her husband. Some days Tamsyn was pretty sure that Marlena was one hundred percent right. It was different for Marlena, though, wasn't it? Marlena had been a single mom right from the start. Like Tamsyn, she hadn't planned on getting pregnant, but unlike Tamsyn she had recognized Philip's father right away for what he was: immature, unhelpful. She knew it would be easier to raise her son on her own than to deal with a man-child of a mate. But Tamsyn had always longed for something more—the traditional family unit: the husband, the kid, the house in the suburbs. She had those things—well, if you considered the Poconos the suburbs.

This dream life of hers turned out to not be as great as she had imagined. Was Sean really any better off than

Philip for having a father around? Maybe there were worse things than not having a father figure, like having a father-figure who set a terrible example and was nothing but a transient figure in the background, stepping up every now and again to be a bad influence.

There were only a few donut holes and less than a full cup of lukewarm coffee remaining when Tamsyn grabbed her free breakfast from the snack table. She scarfed down her donut holes, chased them with the bad coffee, and beside Philip and Marlena, set out to beautify this stretch of state highway.

The morning air was cool and the uninsulated work gloves did little to keep Tamsyn's hands warm as they shuffled along, collecting food wrappers and plastic shopping bags snarled in the roadside weeds. A group not far from them found the first tire of the day, but from Tamsyn's past experience, she knew there would be others. She and Marlena talked about a television show they both liked and then about the rumors swirling around about layoffs at work, and whether or not their own positions were safe.

When Philip was a little ways ahead of them, Marlena said, "He's getting an award for that charity drive he organized. The newspaper's going to be there and everything. I asked Cathy if I could have a couple of hours off Wednesday to go, and she said yes."

"Wow," Tamsyn said. "You must be so proud." She hoped her words didn't sound too sarcastic. She meant them, but it seemed like Marlena was always bragging about Philip, like he was some sort of deity. She shouldn't have to feel bad that her son wasn't out there organizing charity drives. Lots of kids didn't spend their time organizing charity drives.

The morning sun finally started to peek through the

cloudy sky and burn off the fog. The dewdrops on the grass sparkled like diamonds in the sunlight. At first glance it looked like just one more sparkling dewdrop, but then Tamsyn realized what she saw on the ground was something else. She reached down and lifted up a sparkling purple jewel—well, a clear plastic case filled with purple glitter and printed with an illustration of a gemstone. Encased inside was an Android phone. Had a volunteer dropped it? But the condensation on the screen made her think it had been laying in the grass at least overnight. How did a phone get here? Could a pedestrian have dropped it? She wouldn't think this busy stretch of road would see much foot traffic, but there must be the occasional walker.

"Score!" Philip yelled. "You found a phone!"

"It's been out here a while," Tamsyn said. "It might not even work."

She pressed the button and was surprised to see the screen come to life. It still had some charge. She let it go back to sleep. The battery wasn't going to last forever, and someone might be able to figure out how to track down the owner from the phone.

"I'll turn it into someone later," Tamsyn said. She shoved it into the pocket in her fleece.

~

Of course she thought of the phone call.

Tamsyn had not told Marlena about the call. It had been over a week ago now, but she had not been able to get it out of her mind.

She didn't normally answer calls from unknown numbers, but she was headed to the library to meet Lisette and knew that Lisette was one of the last people on earth without a cell phone. She might be calling from the library payphone, or she might have borrowed a phone from someone. Maybe she was calling to let Tamsyn know she couldn't make it tonight, or to ask her for a ride. Probably, though, it was someone calling to try and get her to sign up for a credit card or something.

She had to say hello three times, which convinced her it was a telemarketer of some sort, and she was just about to hang up when she heard something, not speaking exactly. It was muffled, but it sounded like someone crying.

"Sean?" Tamsyn said as her heart began to race. "Sean? Is that you?"

She heard sniffling noises, and then what sounded like it might have been the word, "No." It didn't sound like Sean. It sounded like a woman.

"Who is this?" Tamsyn demanded. Then when she didn't hear anything else said, "Sorry, I think you have the wrong number."

"Ken," it sounded like the voice said. It really wasn't clear, and then whatever else this woman was saying was swallowed up by more crying, and then an abrupt silence. Tamsyn pulled the phone away from her ear and saw the call had ended.

What the hell was that about? Had that been one of Ken's floozies? How did they get her number? Maybe it had just been a wrong number. It sounded like the crying woman had said "Ken" but it could have just as easily been "can." Maybe she was trying to say, "Can you help me?"

She held her phone and waited for it to ring again, but it remained silent. She could try calling the number back. Maybe she should call the police. Maybe she should call Ken. In the end, she did nothing.

The strange phone call weighed on her through the

week. Why had the mysterious crying woman called her? Had the woman gotten the help she needed? Half a dozen times she considered calling back the number, but each time she found some excuse not to. Eventually, she convinced herself that the woman was someone who'd had an affair with Ken. Maybe he had broken it off with her, or maybe the woman had discovered that Ken was a married man. She had called Tamsyn in an emotional state, but when Tamsyn picked up she lost her nerve. It was a lot to infer from some tears and a couple of not too-clearly heard words, but Tamsyn let herself believe this was true. After all, she was pretty sure her husband had never given up his cheating ways.

She had considered telling Marlena about the call, but she knew what Marlena would say. Marlena would say that she should march right down to the attorney's office and get the divorce proceedings started. But Tamsyn didn't think divorce was the magic bullet that would make her life better. Wasn't divorce just another version of quitting? And how had that whole quitting thing gone for her in the past?

Now, as the sun finally warmed the air, Tamsyn looked up and realized she had been so lost in thought that she had wandered away from Marlena and Philip. She had drifted further away from the road than the clean-up crew usually ventured, but it was just as well. Even here there was trash strewn in the weeds—plastic shopping bags and windblown junk food wrappers. As she continued the Sisyphean task of cleaning up the garbage, she questioned not only her decision to continue in a marriage that was a long way from the ideal she dreamed of, as well as the fact that more than a week after that call, she hadn't confronted her husband about it.

Her reasoning was that most likely Ken had already

broken it off with the crying woman, and maybe that was a sign that he really did love her, in his own weird Ken way. He was trying to do the right thing as a husband, even if he did sometimes slip up. After all, didn't everyone make mistakes? A part of her recognized this as rationalizing, as the same sort of thinking that had kept her locked inside her loveless marriage.

She bent down to pick up what at first appeared to be another food wrapper, but when she moved aside the weeds she saw it was an entire garbage bag. People were such pigs. She supposed she could just move this bag to the side of the road with the other bags that the volunteers had already filled so that it could be picked up by the truck in the afternoon. So she tugged at the bag in the weeds to move it out to the road, and was surprised at the weight of the contents.

Moving the bag released a foul odor, and she was reminded of last year when someone had found a dead and partly decomposed raccoon during the cleanup. She didn't want to know what was in the bag, but when she made another attempt to move it, the plastic tore and something spilled out the side.

It was not a raccoon.

3

Tamsyn stared at what had spilled out of the bag in confusion. A voice in her head told her it was a doll, but it was too big to be a doll. The voice said it was a mannequin, but mannequins did not bleed. No, what she was looking at was a human arm, part of an arm. It was slender and pale. Near the wrist was a pretty tattoo, a purple butterfly. Where the hand should have been was a bloody, mangled mess.

Tamsyn staggered away from the severed arm. She felt a churning storm inside her, and squatted down in the weeds as her meager breakfast made a repeat appearance. She was drenched in sweat, though the air was hardly hot. Why had she drifted away from Marlena? If she was still with Marlena this wouldn't have happened. She wouldn't have found the bag with the body. That voice in her head said it might just be an arm, but she had tried to lift that bag and it was heavy. It was more than just an arm. This thought made her stomach heave again, but she swallowed down the bile.

She stood up on shaky legs and tried to wave to catch Marlena's attention, but her friend wasn't looking this way. No one was.

Tamsyn licked her lips and whispered a feeble, "Help." She would have to do better than that. She took a deep breath, and repeated her appeal in a quavering voice, "Help!" Better, but not loud enough to be heard over the cars passing on the road. She felt drained, but she forced herself to suck in a mouthful of air and scream as if her life depended on it.

This time they heard her. She felt faint and leaned back against a tree as she watched Marlena, Philip and a few of the other volunteers running toward her.

4

Tamsyn watched a police officer string up yellow tape between two trees. The area where she had found the trash bag was now a crime scene. The police had erected a small tent where the bag had been found and a crew in white suits with hats and booties were combing the weeds, looking for pieces of evidence.

She'd already given her statement to the police—everything she could remember.

Clean-up Day was officially over. The majority of the litter crew volunteers had departed, their bags of trash abandoned at the side of the road would now be combed through by the police, in case anything they'd picked up was actually evidence.

From where she sat in a spot in the grass, the whole scene looked surreal, like something out of a movie, maybe a science fiction one, with the suited cops combing the weeds. Marlena walked across the field toward her and handed Tamsyn a plastic bottle of water.

"How are you holding up?" Marlena asked.

"I'm okay," Tamsyn said. It was what she had told the police too. She felt if she kept repeating it, the words would come true.

"Why don't you let me drive you home?" Marlena said.

"No, my car is here. I'll just drive myself home," Tamsyn said.

Philip, who had been studying the police in the distance, piped up, "I can drive Mrs. Blake's car. I have my permit."

"No, you're not driving her," Marlena said. "Couldn't one of your neighbors drive Ken over?"

It was a reasonable suggestion, but Tamsyn knew this would never happen. Philip and Marlena began to bicker about him wanting to drive Tamsyn home. Tamsyn stood up and brushed some grass and leaves off her jeans. She swigged a little bit more water from the bottle Marlena had handed her.

"I can drive myself," Tamsyn said. "I'm okay."

Her car felt oppressively hot. It had been baking in the sun in the parking lot. She stripped off her fleece jacket and shoved it into the backseat then rolled down the window, hoping the fresh air might revive her. She felt dizzy but she didn't know how much of that was the heat and how much of that was what had happened in the past hour or so.

She could not get the image of the arm out of her head. Who did it belong to? What was her name? How had she ended up here in a trash bag at the side of the road? Tamsyn felt connected to the mystery woman. More than that. She felt responsible for her. Though she had given the police answers to all of their questions, they had given her none.

She drove home in a disconnected state. Part of her felt like it was still back there in the field, standing beside the remains of the woman in the garbage bag.

5

Tamsyn parked her car in the driveway in front of the garage. Ken had made vague promises about cleaning out the cluttered garage so that they could actually use it to store their cars, but nothing ever came of it, and the garage only grew more and more cluttered with cast-off items. As she stepped across the driveway to the house's side door. she could feel some remnants of adrenaline still surging through her.

Her hand shook as she tried to put her key into the side door's lock. It took her a few extra seconds to complete the routine task. As she opened the door into the kitchen, the aroma of canned chili and Tabasco sauce greeted her. Ken was at the counter, carelessly dumping chili from a small pot into a cereal bowl. Red sauce splattered on the counter and she couldn't help but watch as one drip spilled down the front of the cabinets.

"You're home early," Ken said. "Did you run out of trash to clean up?"

"They had to shut the clean-up down early," she said. "A dead body was found." The words felt like they were being spoken by someone else. She only felt half there. Her other half was back there in the field with the woman in the plastic trash bag. Then she added, "I found her. Ken, it was awful."

Did she tell him that because she wanted sympathy? Tamsyn wasn't sure, but if so, she should have known better than to expect any from her husband.

"Well, it serves you right going out there and picking up garbage like some damn inmate," Ken said.

It reminded her of his comments earlier, when she was trying to wake Sean up, and even though she didn't agree with him, she felt grateful for her husband's opposition to the litter clean-up because it had kept Sean safe at home. The day had been brutal, but it would have been immeasurably worse if Sean had been there. What if Sean had been the one to find the body? No, she didn't even want to think about that.

"Where's Sean?" Tamsyn asked.

"In his room, I think," Ken said. He shrugged. "So, what was it, some hitchhiker that got hit by a car?"

It took her a moment to realize he meant the body.

"No, it was a woman," Tamsyn said. "Someone cut her into pieces and put her in a garbage bag. I saw her arm, coming out of the bag and I thought it was a mannequin, but then I saw the butterfly tattoo on her arm and there was blood, a bloody stump."

"Jesus, Tams, I'm about to eat my lunch here? Do you mind?" He made a grossed-out face to drive home his point. Then he took his bowl of chili and headed into the living room. She could hear the television on in there—a baseball game by the sound of it.

She stared at the mess he had left behind on the counter. On another day she might have asked him if he had any intention of cleaning it up, but she knew there was no point. Ken made a mess of things. That was what he did. He made a mess of their marriage. If she wasn't going to call him out on that, what was the point of calling him out on some spilled chili?

Instead she went over to the cabinet beneath the sink to retrieve the spray bottle of cleaner. She was surprised when she lifted up the bottle. It felt nearly empty. Hadn't she opened a new one just a week or so ago? Well, that was par for the course too, wasn't it? Someone was forever using up something and then not bothering to tell her about it so she could put it on her grocery list. Instead she would go to butter her bagel and find the butter dish empty or be forced to run to the over-priced convenience store down the road when she learned some ingredient for the meal she was making had been entirely consumed.

SUNDAY

I

STATE POLICE DETECTIVE Derek Patterson led her to the small, windowless interview room at the state police barracks.

"Thank you for agreeing to come here," he said. "There were just a few questions I wanted to ask you. So that we can get things squared away."

"Of course," she said. "I'm happy to help."

She was glad to get out of the house, and she was a bit excited to be helping out with an actual police investigation —not just any investigation, but a murder investigation. It made her feel special and important. She felt a sense of obligation about the whole thing, not just because this was the right thing to do. She owed it to the mystery woman to see this thing through to the end, to make sure that justice prevailed.

Detective Patterson had a yellow legal pad with some questions written on it and he began to read these off to her, jotting down her answers as she spoke.

A lot of these were questions she had already answered yesterday, when the uniformed police officers who had responded to the initial 911 call had shown up at the clean-up and taken her statement. Had she noticed anything unusual near the bag? Could she walk them through what had happened leading up to her discovery? That sort of thing.

She told him what she had told them yesterday. She saw the trash bag laying in the field, assumed it was just a bag of garbage, went to lift it, but it was too heavy, and then the arm spilled out.

She could not get that arm out of her head—the pale skin, the tattoo, the bloody mess at the end. She had questions of her own. Who was the woman? What had happened to her? How had she wound up in a trash bag at the side of the road?

When Detective Patterson was done with his questions, she asked her own. "Do you know her name?" she asked.

He looked up from his notes, surprised. "No, not yet," he said. "We're still working on making a positive identification."

"But can't you just check her fingerprints?" she asked.

Detective Patterson hesitated before answering, but finally said, "That only works if she's already in our system, and, well . . . " His voice trailed off. She looked at him expectantly. He fiddled with his pen and seemed to weigh whether or not he would continue. Then said, "And we don't have any fingerprints to work with. We have not, as yet, found her hands."

A gust of wind blew Tamsyn's hair into her face as she stepped out of the police station. She tucked it behind her ear just before someone shoved a microphone in her face. She looked up, startled to see the reporter and the video camera looking at her expectantly.

"What can you tell us about the victim?" the reporter asked. She was young with dark hair and pale skin. "Were you the one who found the body? Do you know the name of the victim?"

Tamsyn felt like a deer frozen in the middle of the road as a large truck bore down on her. She stammered for a good thirty seconds or so before she summoned enough composure to be able to answer the questions. She tried to keep her voice steady as she told her story to the reporter. In the watchful eye of the video camera, Tamsyn felt more nervous than she had speaking to the police detective.

2

Tamsyn left the police station feeling dissatisfied. She still didn't have answers to her questions. She didn't know who the woman was, and it was eating away at her.

She didn't drive straight home. Instead, she took a detour and found herself driving past the field where she had found the woman's body in the bag.

She put her hazards on and pulled over onto the shoulder of the road. The tent was still set up in the field. The yellow police tape fluttered in the breeze. A handful of police officers were working in the field. She watched them. She wondered if they had found any other clues in the surrounding area. Perhaps they had found the missing hands.

The thought made her shudder. Who had done this to this woman and why? She sat there for several minutes just watching, thinking, pondering how a person could be reduced to pieces, reduced to trash, dumped into a bag. It was hard for her to get her head around. She started her car back up but then noticed something. Someone else was watching the police as well.

A slim black man stood maybe fifty yards away from her at the side of the road watching the police working. No, not just watching. She noticed he had a phone in his hand and was filming the activity going on in the field. He turned for a moment and looked back toward her car. She let out a gasp.

It wasn't a stranger. It wasn't a man at all. It was Philip. What was he doing here?

Without thinking, she threw open her door. A horn blared. She quickly shut the door as a car sped past. She checked her mirror before she reopened the door and stepped out.

"Philip!" she called. "What are you doing here?"

Philip fiddled with the phone before sticking it in his pocket. He began to walk in her direction.

"Hi, Mrs. Blake," Philip said when he reached her. "I was filming the police for my YouTube channel."

"You have a YouTube channel?" Tamsyn asked.

"Yeah," he said, "I report on local news."

"Well, let me give you a lift home," Tamsyn said. She thought of a few seconds earlier when her door was nearly ripped off by a passing car. "It's not really safe for you to be hanging out here at the side of the road."

"Thanks," Philip said. "I was done filming anyway."

"The television news just interviewed me outside the police station," Tamsyn said. "If you wanted, you could interview me, too."

"That's okay," Philip said. "I have enough stuff to use."

Tamsyn couldn't help but feel a little hurt. She was getting used to this fifteen minutes of fame, and she was sure she could be more composed and less nervous when Philip interviewed her than when the real reporter had. If nothing else, Philip's interview would have been good practice for her, so that she could be better prepared when she spoke to the next reporter who wanted her story.

As she drove him back home, Tamsyn peppered Philip with questions about his YouTube channel. Apparently, he was interested in a career in journalism and had hopes that the channel would help him get into a good college program.

It made her think of Sean. Had Sean ever once said anything about college or mentioned what kind of career he was considering? What exactly had she done wrong to end up with such an apathetic, unmotivated son? Did Marlena just luck out with Philip, or was this perfect specimen of a teenage boy the result of mothering skills that Tamsyn simply didn't possess?

Philip must have texted his mother, because Marlena was there in the driveway waiting for them when Tamsyn pulled in. Philip gave her a quick wave before rushing into the house to edit his video.

Tamsyn didn't get out of the car, but she rolled down the window to say, "I had no idea he had a YouTube channel."

"I think I preferred it when he was just writing articles

for the school paper, but I guess this is what all the kids are doing these days."

Not all the kids, Tamsyn thought, but she kept her mouth shut.

"Anderson Cooper, look out," Tamsyn said with a laugh.

"You know they used something he filmed on one of the local stations, it was when that big tree came down near the library," Marlena says. "Gave him credit and everything."

"Impressive," Tamsyn said.

"Did I tell you he's getting an award?" Marlena asked.

Tamsyn hoped her smile didn't look as fake as it felt when she said, "You did say something about that."

"They're having a ceremony at the school and everything," Marlena said.

Tamsyn felt her face grow hot. There was a fine line between proud mama and rub-it-in-your-face mama and Marlena tended to cross it fairly often.

"Huh," Tamsyn said.

"Yeah, well I just hope he can somehow parlay this into a college scholarship," Marlena said. "You know what I'm saying?"

Tamsyn nodded. She just hoped Sean could get into a college. She didn't dare to dream about scholarships, though there was no way they would be able to pay for his education without some sort of assistance.

"Hey, what were you doing out by the park, anyway?" Marlena asked.

"I had to go answer some questions at the police station. Basically the same stuff I told them yesterday. I was just on my way back."

"Were you taking the scenic route home?" Marlena asked.

"I had to run a few errands," Tamsyn lied.

How could she explain that the reason she went that way was because she felt a responsibility to a dead woman she'd never met?

3

When she arrived home, Sean was in the kitchen, rummaging through the pantry.

"Do we have any Doritos?" Sean asked.

"I think you finished them up," Tamsyn said. "Hey, I have an idea. Why don't you help me make something for dinner? You always used to love helping me out in the kitchen."

"Yeah, like, when I was five," Sean said.

"Come on, it would be fun," Tamsyn said. "Maybe we should look into some different culinary arts programs. There's some good schools for that. Doesn't that sound like fun?"

"What the hell, Mom?" Sean said.

"I just saw Philip. I gave him a ride home. Did you know he has his own YouTube channel? Some sort of local news thing. They used one of his videos on the television news. He's getting an award for a charity thing he did, Marlena said," Tamsyn added.

"Philip's a dork," Sean said.

"Hey, don't talk like that," Tamsyn said.

She felt a bit like a hypocrite because she'd thought the same thing even if she hadn't spoken it out loud. But so what. What was wrong with being a dork?

"Yeah, well, he's probably going to get a college scholarship out of this," Tamsyn continued. "Have you even thought about college?"

"What do you even care? It's not like you went to college," Sean said.

"I went to college!" Tamsyn yelled. What she didn't add was that she didn't finish, but that wasn't her fault was it? "I went to college," she said again.

But she was losing her audience. Sean shrugged at her. He walked out of the kitchen with a plate piled with junk food.

~

Tamsyn was twenty again, sitting in her English professor's office. She had gone to ask for yet another extension on a paper that was due. Professor Hart took his reading glasses off, wiped a hand over his face and did his best to give her a sympathetic look.

"Maybe this isn't working out for you," Professor Hart said. "Don't take this the wrong way, but sometimes it's not possible to do it all."

Tamsyn was silent. Beside her, infant Sean stirred in his baby carrier. Had it been foolish of her to think she could handle being a full-time student and a new mom? She didn't think that was the case. Ken's own academic pursuits seemed not to have been affected at all by the arrival of the baby, but then Ken seemed not to have been affected at all by the arrival of the baby. She was the one getting up in the middle of the night when Sean cried. She was the one who had to adjust her schedule to take care of Sean or worry about finding someone who could. Ken was blissfully unaware of all of this.

What she needed to do was talk to Ken. What she

needed to do was lay down some ground rules. If they both took equal responsibility, then there was no reason they both couldn't go to school full-time.

"I just need to work some things out with my boyfriend," Tamsyn said. "It's been rough for us adjusting, but once we get a schedule worked out everything will be much better."

"Yes, yes I'm sure that's the case," Professor Hart said. "But in the meantime, I think I'll have to give you an incomplete for this course."

"No, I can do it. I can make up the work," Tamsyn said.

"The end of the semester is only two weeks away," her professor said. "You're weeks behind on the work."

It took the wind out of her sails—that conversation with her professor. She tried to talk to Ken that night, but she felt defeated before she even began. Ken complained that she was babbling and that he was swamped with work.

"But that's what I'm saying," Tamsyn said. "I'm swamped too. I can't do everything myself."

"Your hormones are all out of whack. That's what this is really about," he said.

"This is not about hormones!" she yelled. She hadn't meant to yell—not only did it play into Ken's stupid comment about her being hormonal, but her voice was loud enough to wake the sleeping baby.

"Ugh," Ken said. "There he goes again."

"You should go check on him, rock him back to sleep," she said.

"Do you even listen to a word I say?" he asked. "I'm swamped. I don't have time to be singing lullabies."

"I don't have the time either!" she yelled. She knew if she walked away from this argument, it would be as good as surrendering, but Sean's cries had amped up a notch. He was full-out screaming now, and it broke her heart to hear him so distressed. "This isn't done," she said, before she ran to get him from the closet they had turned into a nursery. As she left, Ken stuck a pair of headphones on, signaling the end of the conversation and, she knew from experience, the end of any conversation that evening.

When the semester ended two weeks later, her transcript was littered with incompletes. She meant to make up the work, she meant to move forward, but motivation became as rare as a full night's sleep. It wasn't like she made a formal decision to drop out. Her college career ended quietly while she was busy trying not to think about all the things she had messed up.

4

T here was a teaser promo before the eleven o'clock news. The perky newscaster said, "Tonight, a grisly discovery along a busy Poconos roadway." Tamsyn normally read while Ken watched the local news, but today she set her book on the nightstand beside her, and swatted at her husband on his side of the bed.

"Turn the volume up," she said, "I don't want to miss anything."

Ken grumbled but nudged the volume up a few degrees.

The news story began with a reporter standing on the side of the road, near where Tamsyn found the body, explaining to the public the details, then suddenly they cut to the interview with her outside of the police station.

"My God, couldn't you at least have run a brush through your hair before the cameras started rolling?" Ken asked. The day had been breezy and her hair was a little askew, though Tamsyn didn't think it looked that bad.

"Shh," she said.

"I'm just saying it's embarrassing, okay?" Ken said. "I mean, look at you. You look like a homeless person or something."

Her interview was over before it began, and they cut back to the news studio, where the woman newscaster urged viewers to call a hotline if they had any information for police on the identity of the unknown woman, or any details about the crime, before moving on to talking about a car wreck that had happened on the turnpike extension.

Ken's remarks stung, but Tamsyn was used to them by now. She was more annoyed that he talked through her interview instead of just letting her watch it.

"You know what's embarrassing," she said. "Embarrassing is being married to someone who can't keep his dick in his pants for five freaking minutes."

"Oh, God, here we go," Ken said. "Let's just go ahead and drag out all the ancient history. I don't know, maybe if my wife took better care of herself, I wouldn't have been tempted to go astray."

"Sure, blame me," she said. "Have you looked at yourself in the mirror lately? You don't exactly look the way you did in college either, but you don't hear me complaining."

"What are you talking about?" he asked. "All you do is complain. Like dragging up something that happened years ago."

"I'm not talking about what happened years ago," she said. "I'm talking about last week. I got a phone call from your latest conquest." She wasn't one hundred percent sure that's what the phone call had been, but she decided to run with this anyway.

"I don't know what you're talking about," Ken said. But she noticed the way his expression changed, and the way he looked just a bit paler in the glow from the television.

"You disgust me," she said, before rolling over so she didn't have to look at him. She shut her eyes, but she knew there was no way sleep would find her anytime soon.

MONDAY

I

TAMSYN'S SLEEP had been rough, and it wasn't just because she was angry with her husband. She kept thinking about the woman in the trash bag. She felt like she couldn't rest until she knew who the woman was and why someone had done the things they had to her.

It was why she left for work a few minutes early on Monday morning. The state police barracks were less than a mile from the social security office. She figured she could stop in and check at the station to see if there was any news before she clocked in for the day.

As she walked up the sidewalk toward the front door of the police station, she heard someone call her name. She turned around and saw Detective Patterson striding toward her. He looked immaculate in a fresh gray suit, and she wondered if he was one of those superhuman types who could work seven days a week without growing tired.

"Was there something new you remembered?" he asked as he fell into step beside her and walked with her to the front door. He looked so eager that she wanted desperately to be able to tell him something, but she didn't have any more information for him.

"I was hoping that maybe you had found out her name or something more about her," Tamsyn said. "I haven't been able to sleep."

"It's nothing you need to worry yourself over," Detective Patterson said. "We've got our best and brightest working on this, and I know we'll get to the bottom of things in no time."

He opened the door and held it for her, but she remained on the sidewalk. She had only come to try and find out more information, and if there wasn't any, then she was just wasting her time here.

"Are you sure there wasn't something else you wanted to tell me?" Detective Patterson asked. His eyes seemed to be full of warmth and sympathy when he looked at her, so why did Tamsyn find herself feeling prickly and uncomfortable?

"I have to go to work," Tamsyn said.

"Of course," he said. "But if anything comes to you, anything at all, don't hesitate to call me."

She hurried back to her car, walking so fast she was practically running. She didn't dare look back, sure that if she did she would find the police detective watching her.

She flung herself into her car and slammed the door closed, hitting the button to lock all the doors. She sat there in the parking lot, behind the steering wheel, trying to catch her breath. Her hands shook, and when her phone chimed with a text message she jumped.

With trembling hands she retrieved her phone from her purse. It was a text from Marlena.

Hope everything is ok, it read. *Call or text to let me know.*

She had misjudged how much time she had. She was already a few minutes late.

On my way, she texted back before starting her car and backing out of the parking space.

How could the police not know the mystery woman's name? Surely somebody had to have reported her missing. She was not even five minutes late for work, and Marlena was ready to send out the rescue helicopters.

2

Tamsyn stared at the social security application form in front of her, but she couldn't focus on the neatly written responses to the questions. Instead she kept checking the clock. Her lunch break began in a few minutes, but time seemed to have slowed to a crawl. Though her stomach did growl, it wasn't hunger that made her so clock-obsessed. She had something she needed to do, a phone call she needed to make. It was something she should have done sooner, but her argument last night with Ken had convinced her.

When one o'clock finally arrived, she jumped up from her desk, and Marlena flashed her an amused smile.

"Somebody's hungry," Marlena said. "Come eat with me?"

"Another day," Tamsyn promised. "There's something I need to go do."

Then for the second time that day, she found herself nearly running to her car.

S he should have recorded her phone conversation with the crying woman. There must be some way to do that. If she had a recording, she would have proof that she could shove in Ken's face. There was another solution.

She could call the number back. It was still there in her history, and not all that far back. It had only been a week since she'd received the call. Tamsyn munched on the crackers from the packet she had brought along for lunch as she scrolled through her recent phone calls.

The call from the crying woman hadn't been the first indication that Ken hadn't kept his promise to be faithful, but it made Tamsyn feel stupid and ashamed. How had she failed so badly at marriage?

The number from the unknown caller was local, in the same 570 area code, anyway. Her finger trembled as she hovered over the number. Maybe she should just send a text message. A text would be easier, but a call quicker. Before she lost her nerve, she tapped the screen to dial the number.

She held the phone to her ear and waited, and a few seconds later she heard a phone start to ring, but not in her ear. This was coming from somewhere else. Did Sean leave his phone in the car again? She quickly ended the call. She looked into the backseat and saw the fleece jacket she'd left there Saturday—the fleece jacket, which still had the cell phone she'd found in the pocket.

With everything that had happened since picking up that phone, she had forgotten all about it. Her heart raced as she grabbed the jacket and fumbled the phone out of the pocket. It was a coincidence that it was ringing at the same time she was making a call. It had to be. To confirm this, she called the unknown number again, and this time she watched as the display on the found phone lit up with the notification of an incoming call, and of course, the incoming call was from her own phone. She ended the call and dropped both phones on the passenger seat as if they were on fire.

"How?" Tamsyn said aloud to the empty car.

She tried to remember where exactly she'd found the phone on Saturday. It was in the damp grass at the side of the road. She thought it was close to the road, but she wasn't sure. Philip and Marlena were with her when she found it, which meant it couldn't have been that close to the trash bag. She was on her own when she discovered the dreadful bag. No, the phone probably belonged to one of the other volunteers. Ken was probably having an affair with one of them. It was the only reasonable explanation.

She should contact the clean-up coordinator and ask if anyone reported a cell phone missing. It would be her opportunity to contact Ken's little sidepiece directly. Was this what she wanted? Tamsyn wasn't sure. Instead, she placed her phone back in her purse and the found phone in her glove compartment. She finished her unsatisfying lunch in silence.

3

Marlena ambushed Tamsyn as she stepped in the back door of the social security office.

"Is everything okay?" Marlena asked—or more like demanded. "Why were you eating lunch out in your car?"

Tamsyn wondered if Marlena had been watching her.

"I had some phone calls to make," Tamsyn said.

"Hey, that reminds me," Marlena said. "Did you ever turn in that cell phone you found the other day?"

"Yeah," Tamsyn lied.

"Because I had a thought, what if that phone could have belonged to the dead woman, or maybe to the person who killed her? It could be evidence."

"It wasn't really anywhere near where the body was," Tamsyn said.

"Yeah it was," Marlena said. "It was right in the same area."

"Well, it didn't have anything to do with the dead woman," Tamsyn said.

"You don't know that," Marlena said. "She could have dropped it when she was trying to get away from her murderer."

Tamsyn didn't want to hear this. She felt like sticking her fingers in her ears and saying, "I can't hear you. La la la," like Sean used to do when he was younger and misbehaving. But of course she couldn't do this. The best she could do was try to tune her coworker out.

"I turned it into the police," Tamsyn lied again. "That's why I was late this morning. I dropped it off at the state police barracks." She felt like adding this detail made it only a white lie. After all, she *had* been at the state police barracks this morning. Still, Marlena frowned at this, as if she didn't believe Tamsyn.

"And they kept it for evidence?" Marlena asked.

Tamsyn wanted this conversation to be over. She wondered if Marlena really had been spying on her while she ate her sad little lunch out in her car. Had Marlena seen her holding the two phones?

"No, they said it belonged to one of the other volunteers at the clean-up," Tamsyn said. It was a stupid lie that she regretted immediately. It would be too easy for busybody

Marlena to find out it wasn't true. "They just called while I was on my lunch break to let me know."

Tamsyn didn't give Marlena a chance to ask any more questions. She brushed past her to get back to her desk so she could finish processing the morning's paperwork.

TUESDAY

I

TUESDAY MORNING, Tamsyn left for work a half hour earlier. For some reason Ken didn't have to go into work until the afternoon, which meant he would spend the morning hanging around the house pestering her, and she liked to relax with a cup of coffee and a book in the morning before she headed out. So, she told her husband she had an early morning staff meeting, then drove herself to Panera, so she could enjoy her book and coffee in peace. She never did crack open her book, though.

The table she snagged had somebody's left-behind newspaper on it. It was that day's copy of the *Pocono Record*, and the headline caught her attention: POLICE IDENTIFY WOMAN FOUND IN TRASH BAG. She was surprised that Detective Patterson didn't call her to let her know about this development. It felt like he owed her that courtesy after all the questions she had answered for him. Tamsyn knew she wasn't part of the investigation, but if they were going to inform a reporter at the newspaper, couldn't they at least have told her what was going on?

Jillian Nelson. That was the woman's name. The article gave few details about who she was and gave the vague reassurance that the police had a few possible leads in their murder investigation. There was not much meat to the story, so Tamsyn's eyes went back to the first paragraph. She felt dizzy as she stared at the letters spelled out in black print: Jillian Nelson. A name changed everything.

That had certainly been the case when she was pregnant with Sean.

Her parents were opposed to the idea of her going through with the pregnancy.

"You're young," her mother said. "You have your whole life ahead of you. You have plenty of time to start a family. Now's not the right time."

"But what if it is?" Tamsyn asked. "What if it's fate? Maybe this is meant to be."

She was home from college for the weekend. At dinner the night before she had worked up the courage to tell her parents she was pregnant and was going to be moving in with her boyfriend Ken. They both did their best not to yell at her, but she could read the disappointment on their faces.

Now she sat at the kitchen table while her mother loaded the dishwasher with their dirty breakfast dishes, trying not to bristle as her mother lectured her.

"What's meant to be is you're meant to get your degree, start your career, and when you're married and have a house of your own you're meant to start having babies," her mother said as she shoved the last coffee mug into the dishwasher and slammed the door shut. It was the closest she had come so far to losing her temper.

"I'm still going to get my degree, I'm still going to start my career," Tamsyn said. "None of that's going to change."

Her mother sighed, and stared out the kitchen window as if she couldn't bear to face her daughter.

"I don't think you can begin to appreciate what's involved in being responsible for another human being," her mother said.

"I'm a grown woman," Tamsyn said. She hadn't shouted, but she had raised her voice. "I can be responsible for a child."

"Right," her mother said in a sarcastic tone. "Because it was all that responsibility of yours that got you into this mess in the first place."

Tamsyn stormed out of the house. If she could have, she would have gone straight back to school without saying another word to either of her parents, but she didn't have a car. She called Ken and asked if he could come pick her up, but he said he was busy. He didn't seem to understand why she couldn't just have her parents drive her back. In the end, this was what she did. It was a long, chilly car ride.

Over the next few weeks, her mother sent her links to different articles and assorted clinics that performed abortions, but Tamsyn mostly ignored them. Instead she would flip through the pages of the baby name book she had borrowed from the library. She imagined what her son or daughter would be like if it was named Madison, Arthur, Nicole or Paul.

Then her mother surprised her by showing up at the college unannounced. She had made an appointment for Tamsyn at a clinic and drove the two of them there. If Tamsyn was being honest, she felt relieved. From her apartment search with Ken, she had learned that rent was impossibly steep and that nice or even halfway decent apartments did not seem to exist.

The first step at the clinic was for Tamsyn to speak with a counselor. So, she signed in at the front desk and sat down beside her mother in the waiting room.

"You don't have to make a decision today, but I want you listen to what they have to say and consider all of your options," her mother said.

Tamsyn nodded. Across the way from them, a young boy played with a toy car on the floor. He was there with his mother, who looked young. Tamsyn wondered if the woman was pregnant with another baby or just here for a routine gynecological exam. The little boy looked up at Tamsyn and smiled shyly, and suddenly she felt on the verge of crying as she looked at the boy and imagined he was her own son.

It was then that her name was called. Only the woman who called her, the counselor had messed up the pronunciation of her name. "Tam-Sean," it sounded like she said. It was then that Tamsyn knew that she was going to have a boy, and she was going to name him Sean. Despite her mother's request that she listen to everything the counselor had to say, Tamsyn heard very little of it. She had already made up her mind. Her head filled with a vision of holding her infant son in her arms, and the name she knew she would give him, Sean. Once she'd decided on a name, there could be no going back. He had become a real person to her, and nothing could change her mind.

∼

The feeling that washed over her in Panera as she stared at Jillian's name in the newspaper reminded her of that feeling that had washed over her in that clinic waiting room all those years ago. Just as giving a name to her unborn child made him real, and so too did giving a name to a dead body she'd found in a trash bag. It was no longer just a dead body. Her name was Jillian, and she was a real person who had a mother and a father, who had hopes and dreams. Tamsyn didn't know the first thing about Jillian Nelson, but she knew this: she didn't deserve to wind up dead and dismembered in a trash bag.

When she'd named her unborn child, she'd felt a sudden sense of responsibility for the little human growing inside her. Learning Jillian Nelson's name made her feel responsible for this unfortunate woman. It was too late to save her, but sitting at that little table, her forgotten coffee cooling in front of her, Tamsyn made a silent promise to Jillian.

I will not let them forget you. I will not let the monster who did this to you get away with it.

2

It was late morning, and Tamsyn was caught up with her paperwork. The applicant scheduled for eleven had not shown up, and so Tamsyn made use of this little windfall of time by doing some internet sleuthing.

She typed the name "Jillian Nelson" into the Google search box and pressed enter. The search engine populated the page with a series of links, most looked to be sites aimed at tracking down addresses and phone numbers for a fee, but Tamsyn didn't get the chance to investigate further. Tamsyn heard the telltale jingle of a charm bracelet as Marlena stepped up behind her workstation. Tamsyn quickly x-ed out of Google. Maybe a little too quickly. It probably looked suspicious.

"How are you doing?" Marlena asked.

"Good," Tamsyn said. "How are you?"

"You were late again this morning. You sure everything's all right?"

Despite leaving a half hour early, Tamsyn had lost track of time while having her coffee and ended up being few minutes late. It wasn't really a big deal.

"Ken had the morning off," Tamsyn said. "With all his interruptions it took me twice as long to get ready."

"Well, that wouldn't be a problem if you took my advice and left the bastard," Marlena said. "I was just thinking that maybe you were still a little freaked out about finding that body."

"Jillian," Tamsyn said. She didn't know why she felt the need to say the name out loud. Maybe it had something to do with that silent promise she made.

"What?" Marlena asked.

"Did you see the news?" Tamsyn asked. "The police have identified her as Jillian Nelson."

"Oh, okay," Marlena said. Tamsyn was annoyed that Marlena didn't seem to care at all about this development. She reasoned that it was different for Marlena. After all, Marlena wasn't the one who found the body. She didn't have the same connection to Jillian that Tamsyn did. "Hey, you know I was talking to Chris who coordinates the volunteers for the clean-up," Marlena continued, "and he said that no one had reported to him that they lost a phone."

"Well, they must not have reported it to him," Tamsyn said. "Maybe they just contacted the police."

"That's weird, though, isn't it?" Marlena asked. "Why wouldn't they say something to Chris? I mean, if you hadn't found that dead body and been all distracted, you probably would have turned it into Chris."

"Maybe the same thing happened to them," Tamsyn said. "They were distracted by all the excitement, and forgot all about reporting their phone missing." She wished Marlena would just forget about the damn phone already. "Look, a woman's been murdered. There are more important things than some missing cell phone."

"But that's what I mean," Marlena said. "I can't help but feel that it might have some connection to the murder. Just because the phone belonged to a volunteer, doesn't mean that they aren't also the murderer. I mean, if they were a regular clean-up volunteer they would be pretty familiar with that area. So, maybe that's why they chose that spot to dump that woman's body."

"Jillian," Tamsyn said, reminding her that "that woman" had a name. "I don't think what you're saying makes sense. If they were a volunteer, why would they dump her there if they knew the clean-up was going to happen? They must have known that someone would find her."

Tamsyn heard someone clear their throat and looked up to see her boss, Cathy, standing beside her workstation. She crossed her arms over her chest and gave Tamsyn and Marlena her best schoolmarm look.

"I do hope this is a work-related discussion we're having, ladies," Cathy said.

"Of course," Marlena said in a fake sweet voice.

"Because if you're bored and looking for something to do, I'm sure I can accommodate you," Cathy said.

Marlena waited until Cathy began to walk away, then made a face at her retreating back, before spinning back around to Tamsyn to say, "I guess we'll have to continue talking over lunch today."

"Can't," Tamsyn said. The last thing she wanted was to continue this conversation with Marlena. "I've got something I've got to do."

"Again? Are your sure everything's all right?"

"Positive," Marlena said, and she grabbed a piece of paper from her desk and pretended that it was something important that she had to deal with.

3

Tamsyn's hands shook as she opened the glove box to retrieve the other cell phone. She would check out the information on the phone. In the settings or somewhere it would have the owner's name, and that name was going to be Monica or Tiffany, or something else, anything but Jillian, and that would be it. She would put the whole ugly mess to bed.

She pressed the button to wake the screen up, but it remained black. She tried again. Nothing. Had she done something wrong? It was an Android phone, not an iPhone like hers. Maybe she didn't know how these worked. She looked for some other button that she should have pressed, but no it wasn't that. The battery had finally worn out. It was probably a miracle that it had lasted as long as it did.

It wasn't the end of the world. Phones could be charged, and as recently as yesterday this one had worked fine. It would still work. She had a charger here in the car, but she quickly realized her mistake. Her charger was for an iPhone. It wouldn't fit.

Marlena's phone was a Samsung. She could ask to borrow Marlena's charger. The conversation from this morning, the one from yesterday too, came back to her. Marlena would want to know what she needed an Android phone charger for. Of course Marlena would think of the phone that Tamsyn had found. Marlena had been a little bit obsessed with it, hadn't she? No, she definitely couldn't ask to borrow Marlena's charger. She would have to go buy one at the store.

Tamsyn checked the time. She decided she probably didn't have time to make it to the store and back without being late. She might have risked it, but she'd already been late this morning and yesterday, and there was Marlena— nosy, busybody Marlena to consider. No, forget it. She would have to wait until after work.

It was six years ago, a week after Sean's birthday. Tamsyn was gathering up dirty clothes to run a load of laundry. She picked up a pair of Ken's pants that had been flung over the chair in their bedroom. She grabbed them, then checked the pockets to make sure she didn't actually ruin a whole load of laundry with a mini chocolate bar or a cherry-flavored cough drop. It had happened before. The one pocket was empty. She reached into the second and her hand closed around something smooth, flat and rectangular. She pulled it out. It was his phone. She stared at it. But no. Had he gotten a new phone?

It was possible he could have. She was surprised he hadn't told her about it, but not that surprised. There were a lot of things Ken didn't tell her. Still, hadn't he had his phone in his hand when he'd left the house fifteen minutes ago to run his errands? She was sure he had.

She hit the button to wake the phone. It was locked with a passcode, but she had known Ken long enough to know that he only had a few numbers and passwords he used to secure his devices and accounts. She tried a couple of strings of numbers before she hit upon the magic sequence. The phone's colorful home screen came to life.

She hesitated, but then curiosity won out. She pulled up the phone's contacts screen, her reasoning being that if this really was Ken's phone she would recognize the contacts. Sean would be there as would she, Ken's parents, his work, his friends. But none of those numbers were there. No, wait, there was his work number, but she wasn't there, nor was Sean, nor his parents, nor any other names that she recognized. Instead, the contacts stored in his phone were female names: Brenda, Sara, Katelyn, Maya, Georgette. She had never heard of any of these women.

There could be an innocent explanation. Maybe the company had issued him this phone. These women could all be work contacts. She shouldn't jump to conclusions. Instead she jumped over to the message app. She read through a couple of strings of texts and decided that these were not work contacts.

The texts consisted mainly of lame pick-up lines on Ken's part and half-assed innuendo on the parts of the assorted women. If you were being generous you could call it clever banter, but Tamsyn wasn't in a generous mood. Then there were the texts that included pictures—graphic, explicit pictures.

Tamsyn sat down on the bed and set the phone down beside her. Her heart was racing and she felt shaky. It wasn't like she hadn't had her suspicions before. Ken always seemed to have work things that took him away from the house at odd times—late on a Friday night, or in the middle of the day on a weekend. In the back of her mind, she'd suspected that couldn't be right. Plus there was all the hanging out he did with his friends. Did she ever see these guys? What grown man spent that much time hanging out with his friends without his wife around? It didn't add up. So, the fact that her husband had not been entirely faithful was not something that came as a surprise.

What unnerved her was how many women there seemed to be. She picked up the phone again, thinking she would wake it and tally up just how many female names were there in his contacts list, but set it back down before she could do this. She didn't want to know. Too many was the answer. She thought of those stupid texts. It was all just some sort of game to him. Did he even care about any of those women? Did he care about anyone?

4

Tamsyn stood in line behind a group of giggling teenagers as loud dance music blared from the speaker above her head. In her hand, Tamsyn held an android phone charger. It was purple, like the phone's glitter case. *Like Jillian's butterfly tattoo*, a voice in her head said.

She paid for the charger and hurried back out to her car to put it to use. Back in her car, still in the store parking lot, she tore the package open and hooked up the phone. Her heart raced as she waited for it to charge.

She tried to distract herself with thoughts about what

she would make for dinner when she got home. Should she stop at the store and pick something up? Did she have enough leftovers in the fridge that she could heat up? Ken liked to make little snide comments when dinner was nothing but leftovers, but she really didn't care.

The phone had enough charge now to wake the screen, and she forgot all about dinner. She left it hooked up to the charger as she woke it up. She didn't know where on the phone to find the phone's owner's info, but she saw a photos app and opened it.

Tamsyn breathed a sigh of relief as she scrolled through photos of people she didn't recognize. There were random photos: a cake, a shoe, a cat. It was all completely innocent stuff. This was just some random woman's lost phone. Some random woman that Ken was probably having an affair with, she reminded herself.

She had looked at how many photos? A dozen? Twenty? It should have been enough, but for some reason she kept scrolling. Her relief melted away in an instant. Tamsyn found herself staring into the eyes of a familiar looking woman. The photo was a selfie taken in a bathroom mirror. Tamsyn saw shampoo bottles, hairspray, a brush, a shower curtain in the background, and also Jillian Nelson. She was almost a spitting image of the photo that had appeared in this morning's Pocono Record story. Still, Tamsyn's mind argued that it was just some woman who looked a lot like Jillian. Her hair was similar and her facial features, but it was just a coincidence. Then Tamsyn spotted the tattoo. It was reflected in the bathroom mirror. The butterfly's purple wings looked darker than Tamsyn remembered, but it was because the lighting was off in the selfie photo. The woman and her tattoo were unmistakable. Tamsyn couldn't stop staring.

When a digital ring broke the silence, Tamsyn let out a yelp and dropped the phone with a start. It fell harmlessly onto her passenger seat. She stared at it, but she realized after a few moments that it wasn't Jillian's phone that was ringing. It was her own.

She did not recognize the number, but it was local. Could it be the police? Tamsyn answered possibly a second or two before it went to voicemail with a breathless hello.

"Tamsyn?" the female voice on the other end said. "Is everything okay? It's Lisette."

"It's Tuesday," Tamsyn said, as she realized her error.

"I'm at the library," Lisette said. "If you were busy, or if something came up it's okay. I understand."

On Tuesdays Tamsyn tutored Lisette McKissack. They had met when Lisette had come in with a blank form to apply for social security disability after being injured at work. Tamsyn could do nothing with a form that hadn't been completed. When Tamsyn questioned her about this, Lisette broke down in tears. She didn't know how to read or write. Tamsyn had broken protocol to meet with Lisette after work hours and help her to fill out the disability form, and then had suggested that she could tutor Lisette in reading and writing basics.

Tamsyn had no formal tutoring experience, and Lisette had no money, but insisted on bringing home-baked goods as payment. Their sessions had begun back before Christmas. Lisette still struggled with writing, but she could read more words than she had ever been able to before. Seeing Lisette's joy brought Tamsyn joy, and she had come to think of the woman who was about a decade older than she was as a friend.

She normally looked forward to her Tuesday evenings at the library with Lisette, but today their meeting had completely slipped her mind. Well, there had been a lot going on. It wouldn't really hurt anything to skip tonight's session. They could catch up next week.

Was that fair to Lisette, though? She was already at the library. She didn't drive, which meant having to take the county bus or beg a relative or neighbor for a ride. Still, Tamsyn wondered if she would really be any good at tutoring tonight. She had too much on her mind, and didn't know if she would be able to focus. Perhaps Lisette had seen her pathetic interview on the news, and she would understand if Tamsyn wasn't able to make it tonight.

And if she didn't go tutor Lisette? Well, she would head home, where she would have to face the challenge of making something for dinner to feed her family. Tuesdays Sean and Ken were left to fend for themselves, which was one reason that Ken always railed about her tutoring sessions. Well, that and the fact that she was doing her tutoring on a volunteer basis and not getting paid.

Tamsyn glanced at the now-sleeping phone beside her. It was entirely possible her husband had been having an affair with a woman who was now in pieces in the county morgue. It was all the motivation she needed.

"I'm on my way," Tamsyn said. "Sorry I'm running late, but I'll be there soon."

"Okay, I'll be waiting here by the pay phone for you," Lisette said. "If you change your mind, just ring back and let me know."

∾

The day after she found her husband's secret cell phone, she called the divorce attorney that regularly advertised in the newspaper. He had some time that afternoon, and she left work early to meet with him for her free consultation.

"I'm going to ask you the same thing I ask all of my clients," he said. "Are you sure this is what you want?"

She nodded her head and started to answer, but he held up a hand to stop her.

"I'm not talking about love and marital accord right now," he continued. "I'm not saying that's not important, but I want to make sure you understand the reality of the situation. Divorce is not pleasant, and I wouldn't advise anyone go through with it before they have a pretty solid plan. Where are you going to live? Are there kids involved? If so, how will custody work out? Will they need to change schools?"

Tamsyn had assumed that she would stay in the house. She would send Ken packing. After all, he was the one who had cheated on her who-knew-how-many times. The lawyer's words woke her up. They lived month to month as it was. There was no way she would be able to afford the mortgage, taxes and household bills on her meager civil servant's salary. She would have to find a smaller place, an apartment in town, maybe. How would that sit with Sean? She didn't want to make him change schools, but it might be tough to find an affordable place in the same school district.

"What about alimony and child support?" Tamsyn asked.

"You may be entitled to both, but from my experience it's not always something you can rely on."

"So, you're saying I might not be able to afford to leave my worthless husband."

"You might not be able to afford not to," the lawyer said. "I just want you to consider everything before you begin the process. This is a huge decision."

She left the lawyer's office in a confused state. On the one hand, she wanted nothing more than to give Ken the boot and wash her hands of him forever. On the other hand, she didn't know if she had what it took both financially and emotionally to start everything over. The first seeds of doubt had been planted.

5

"Something's bothering you," Lisette said.

Tamsyn looked up with a start. She had been lost in her thoughts, a million miles away from the library table where she and Lisette sat. Tamsyn was trying to recall what she had actually heard in that strange phone call she had received last week. Was it possible she had jumped to conclusions? Was it possible that the woman whose body she had found in the trash bag had no connection to Ken?

"It's nothing," Tamsyn said. Lisette raised her eyebrows. She didn't for a second believe Tamsyn's lie.

"Seems like more than nothing," Lisette said.

Tamsyn knew she'd made a mistake coming here tonight. She wasn't in the right frame of mind to be doing any tutoring. She was just wasting her and Lisette's time tonight.

"I'm sorry," Tamsyn said. "I haven't been sleeping well the past few nights."

"Is it your husband?" Lisette asked. Tamsyn almost gasped at Lisette's question before she realized what her student meant. In the past she had vented to Lisette about Ken being unhelpful and critical of her. Lisette had listened and sympathized. Tamsyn was grateful that unlike Marlena, Lisette wasn't always asking her when she was finally going to leave the bastard. So, of course it made sense that Lisette would think that was what was troubling Tamsyn. It was, but not in the way that Lisette meant.

"Have you seen the news?" Tamsyn asked, glad that she caught herself before asking if Lisette, still a struggling reader at best, had read the newspaper. "Did you see the story about the woman whose body was found in a garbage bag?"

Lisette nodded, but didn't say anything.

"Well, I was the one who found the body," Tamsyn continued. "I haven't been able to get it out of my head."

Lisette laid a comforting hand over Tamsyn's. It was a simple gesture, but it brought Tamsyn a little peace.

"It's awful," Lisette said. "I knew her. She didn't deserve that."

"You knew her?" Tamsyn was surprised at how loud her voice sounded in the quiet library. A woman reading a book at a nearby table turned around to glare. Tamsyn ignored her.

"Well, not well or anything," Lisette said. "She lived near me, a couple of years ago, when I was still out in Scranton. Before the accident."

Tamsyn knew that the accident Lisette referred to was the one with the forklift at work. The one that had prevented Lisette from being able to do her job. She had been forced to give up her apartment and had moved in with her sister in East Stroudsburg.

"What was she like?" Tamsyn asked. "She looked pretty in the photo I saw. What sort of person was she? Was she dating anyone?"

Lisette gave her a strange look. It was a weird question. Tamsyn regretted asking it. What sort of normal person on finding a woman dismembered in a trash bag went around asking people about her love life?

"Well, I didn't really know her that well at all," Lisette said. "And I heard that she'd fallen on some hard times. Had some problems with drugs, is what I heard."

Weirdly, this gave Tamsyn hope. She saw her share of drug addicts desperately attempting to file for social security benefits at work. They were a sad and hopeless lot. Jillian's phone call could have been nothing but a last-ditch attempt to get money, some sort of scam or something. It might have been a wrong number. Maybe she had been trying to call a drug dealer. Maybe the drug dealer's name was Ken. The whole thing could be some strange, horrible coincidence.

"Maybe you should head on home. Try to get caught up on that missing sleep," Lisette said.

Tamsyn returned her attention to the library table. She had been a million miles away.

"I'm sorry," Tamsyn said.

"Don't be," Lisette said. "I'm kind of tired tonight, too. I waited in a long line at the career center today."

"You're going back to work?"

"Not working's driving me crazy," Lisette said, then after a pause, "So's living with my sister. Anyway, they're hiring a bunch of entry-level staff for the new juvenile detention facility. I picked up an application."

"That's great," Tamsyn said.

"I'm going to try filling out the application at home, but was thinking maybe you could look it over for mistakes, if I bring it with me next week?"

"Of course," Tamsyn said.

Lisette began to gather up her things, and Tamsyn did the same. She was still only half present. Part of her was scrambling to find scenarios where a desperate, drug-addicted woman could have gotten her phone number to try and scam her out of money. She really needed more information to go on. It would be weird to keep pestering Lisette with questions, wouldn't it? But maybe just one more question would be okay.

They both began to walk together toward the front door of the library.

"I was wondering," Tamsyn began. "Do you think you could give me the address? Where she lived? Where Jillian lived?"

Lisette stopped walking and turned to look at Tamsyn. Had she gone too far in asking for an address?

"Why on earth would you want that?" Lisette asked.

Tamsyn felt herself blush. Standing there in the middle of the library, she couldn't help but feel like people were staring at them. She looked away quickly and for a moment debated saying forget it. Because that's how she had always been, wasn't it? She even imagined the way the words, "forget it," would sound rolling off her tongue, but of course, she could never forget it. That arm in the trash bag would haunt her forever. She would never be able to quite forget that phone conversation with the sad, desperate woman. And really, if she was being honest, when had she ever been able to forget any of the things she had said "forget it" to in the past? Had she forgotten about Ken's infidelities? Had she forgotten about the college degree she never finished?

Tamsyn found her voice, but it wasn't the words "forget it" that spilled from her mouth. "I was just thinking it might help to bring some sort of closure to see where she lived."

Lisette nodded as she considered this. "Yeah, I could see that."

Lisette fished around in her purse then pulled out a pad

of paper and a pen. With her face screwed up in determination, she marked slow, deliberate strokes on the piece of paper to spell out the address. Then she handed the piece of paper over to Tamsyn.

"It's the first time I've ever written a note to someone," Lisette said with a note of awe in her voice.

Tamsyn felt a swelling of pride in her own chest, and then because she didn't know what else to do, she gave her friend a hug.

6

After what felt like hours of tossing and turning, Tamsyn slipped out of bed. The movement did not disturb Ken, who kept on snoring. She felt her way through the dark bedroom, then went downstairs to get a glass of water. As she reached for a glass from the cabinet, something on the top shelf caught her eye--her old "Bearly Awake" mug. She couldn't remember seeing that thing in years. She changed her mind about the water and decided on herbal tea instead. As she sat in the living room, sipping the minty herbal tea from the old novelty mug, a memory of wrapping the mug up in a piece of newspaper came back to her.

Moving out of her dorm room and into an apartment with Ken had seemed like the first step in a whole new life for her. She had been excited and nervous. Her parents thought it was a huge mistake.

Her mother, at least, had showed up to help her pack things up, but her father had stayed home in protest.

"He loves you," her mother stressed as she began loading items from Tamsyn's desk into a plastic milk crate. "He just disagrees with your decision."

"He thinks I'm a child," Tamsyn said. "He can't accept the fact that I'm an adult."

"Well, you'll always be our little girl," her mother said, "but it isn't that simple. We're worried that you haven't thought things through. You know, you could just stay here in the dorm if you wanted."

"I'm not allowed to have a baby here in the dorms," Tamsyn said. Even if she didn't want to move in with Ken, she would have to find an apartment off-campus for herself. She and Ken could barely afford an apartment together. She didn't see how she could swing one on her own. Moving in with Ken just seemed like the better option all around. Tamsyn wrapped her "Bearly Awake" mug—a gift from her roommate— in newspaper and placed it into the plastic milk crate.

"You don't have to go through with having the baby is what I'm saying," her mother said.

"First of all, his name is Sean, and I'm not having an abortion just because some people think a child is an inconvenience."

"There are other options," her mother said with a sigh, as she began removing clothes from Tamsyn's closet and laid them on the bed. "There are organizations that can help find prospective parents who want to adopt. It might be the best thing you can do for the child."

"You think I'm incapable of raising a child?" Tamsyn asked.

"That's not what I'm saying. But you have to think about your future, and your baby's future."

"That's exactly what I'm thinking about," Tamsyn said.

She stormed out of the dorm room and down the hall to the common area. She threw herself down on the stained and torn couch and blinked back the tears in her eyes. Lately every stupid little thing seemed to make her cry. The other night Ken said something about her skirt being too tight and she started bawling. She wondered if it was hormones or her body's attempt to tell her that she was making a huge mistake, because despite what she said to her mother, she wasn't sure whether or not she was doing the right thing.

A few minutes later, her mother came out and found her still sitting on the battered couch.

"You know that I think you're a smart and capable woman, don't you?" her mother asked.

Tamsyn felt a lump in her throat. So, she nodded her agreement.

"Whatever decision you make, I'll support you," her mother continued, "if it's what you really want, but I want to make sure you consider all your options."

Tamsyn nodded again.

"I really want to do this," Tamsyn said. "I want to be a mom."

"Well, then let's go finish packing up your stuff," her mother said.

Tamsyn took another sip of tea, as she sat in her living room, remembering that day nearly seventeen years ago. What if she had followed her mother's advice and given her infant son up for adoption? She felt a stabbing pain in her chest, just thinking about not having Sean around, of not seeing him take his first steps, not watching him get on the school bus on his first day of kindergarten or being there to give him a hug when he was having a bad day. No, she couldn't imagine her life without Sean.

Still, how different would her own life be if she had not had him or if she had given him up? She would have finished college, no doubt. It's unlikely that without the baby she ever would have married Ken. Where would she be working? Where would she be living? It made her dizzy to imagine how different things would have turned out for her. Maybe things would have been much worse for her. Something tragic might have happened.

She could have just as easily wound up in a trash bag at the side of the road. Jillian must have had some what-ifs of her own. Where had her life taken its dark turn? Could one of her what-ifs have saved her from her horrible fate?

The address that Lisette had given her called to her. She got up and rummaged through her purse until she located the scrap of paper. If she went there, would she be able to find out what had led to Jillian's death? Would she be able to find out anything at all?

WEDNESDAY

I

THE TURN-BY-TURN DIRECTIONS that Tamsyn's phone read off to her led her through increasingly shabby neighborhoods. She checked that her doors were locked as she drove and rolled her window nearly all the way up. She hadn't seen any indication that the neighborhood was unsafe, but it made her feel uneasy. At least she was here during daylight hours. Sagging duplexes with peeling paint crowded against each other on the narrow street. The phone announced that she had arrived at her destination, and Tamsyn, already rolling along at a modest speed, slowed to a crawl. She craned her neck up at the building—a four-story brick apartment building that reminded her of the first apartment she had lived in with Ken.

Tamsyn circled the block in search of a parking space. After finding one and parking, she sat behind the wheel, her hands trembling. What did she do now? She had called into work sick in order to drive out to the address Lisette had given her, but now that she was here she wasn't sure what to do. Had she thought that seeing where Jillian lived would be enough? The truth was, she didn't know if Jillian had even still lived there. Lisette had moved away nearly a year ago. Jillian could have moved in the meantime. Maybe if she took a walk around the neighborhood, she would see someone who knew Jillian, who could answer her questions. She looked out her window at the run-down surroundings. Did she really want to be approaching strangers in this neighborhood and asking them all sorts of questions?

You owe it to her, a voice in her head said. Yes, she decided. She needed to be brave. This was something she had to do for Jillian.

She stepped out of the car and hit the automatic door lock button on the door before quickly closing it. She realized her error almost immediately. She looked back through the window at her purse sitting on her passenger seat with her car key neatly clipped to the handle. She was surprised to see Jillian's cell phone on the seat beside her purse. Why hadn't she put that away in the glove box? She felt in her jacket pocket, but her own phone must have been in her purse.

Panic rose in her chest. She was locked out of her car in a strange, not-so-safe looking neighborhood. How could she have made such a stupid mistake? She tried to keep her thoughts from spiraling out of control so that she could come up with a plan.

Hadn't she passed a gas station a few blocks back? She tried to remember what direction that had been. She would walk there. They would have a pay phone. She knew there was a card safely locked in her glove compartment with a roadside assistance number printed on it. Never mind, she would just call a local locksmith and they would send someone out to help her. How much would it cost? Would she have enough cash to cover it? If Ken saw that she had used their credit card to pay a locksmith in Scranton, he would have questions. Well, one thing at a time. She couldn't worry about that now. First, she had to find that gas station.

She began to walk in what she thought was the right direction but stopped. She had driven partway around the building to find a parking space. She had come into this neighborhood on a different road and from a direction. She tried to mentally retrace her route, then looked around to get her bearings. She began walking again, but only made it a few more steps before she saw someone she recognized. She froze. That panicked feeling rose up again in her chest.

"Tamsyn?" Detective Patterson seemed as surprised to see her as she was to see him. He cocked his head at her like a dog desperately trying to understand what its owner was saying. "What are you doing here?" he asked.

"I--" she glanced back towards her car, as if the answer was there. Of course, it made sense that the police were here. They would be investigating Jillian's home and neighborhood. Why hadn't she thought of that when she got the address from Lisette? That gave her an idea. "I was here to do a favor for a client." She wasn't sure why she had used the word "client." It felt all wrong rolling off her tongue. "Well, a friend," she corrected. "I met her through work. She used to live here. She left behind some things when she moved. I'm here to see if the landlord is still holding onto them for her and pick them up."

The lies came out too easily, but the police detective was still studying her with what felt like suspicion.

"The landlord lives here?" Detective Patterson asked.

"I'm supposed to call him," Tamsyn said.

"Well, okay," he said, and Tamsyn suddenly saw the beauty of her lie.

"I've locked my phone and my keys in my car," she said.

A couple of minutes later, Detective Patterson stood beside a young uniformed police officer who used a tool to reach through Tamsyn's still cracked open window to reach the door lock button.

"Lucky you left the window open a crack," Detective Patterson said to her.

"Lucky I ran into you," she said.

The uniformed officer let out a little grunt as he twisted his hand to reach the lock button, and then she heard the magical sound of her doors unlocking.

Detective Patterson opened the door for her and stood beside it.

"There's your phone," he said, nodding toward the passenger seat where Jillian's phone sat in plain view.

Tamsyn stepped over to the car. She reached across to the passenger seat and picked up Jillian's phone with a shaking hand. The uniformed officer was headed back to his patrol car, but Detective Patterson still stood beside her car. He was waiting for her to make that call. He didn't believe her stupid lie.

Tamsyn was ready to use the excuse that the phone's battery was dead and she needed to charge it, when she accidentally woke the screen up. She almost yelled out in surprise, but she reminded herself that there was nothing incriminating about the home screen. If this was her phone, she could go to the contacts and call a random number where she knew she would get voicemail, but she was scared to pull up the contacts on Jillian's phone. The police detective watched her like a hawk.

Just as she was about to use the excuse that she had never added the landlord's number to the phone, and had to find the piece of a paper she had written it down on, the phone began to ring. This time she couldn't help but jump in surprise.

"What's that?" Detective Patterson asked, and that's when she realized that it was her phone, the one still in her purse that was ringing.

"My phone," Tamsyn said. "My other phone, I mean."

It was a perfectly timed distraction. She set Jillian's phone down on the driver's seat and reached in to dig her ringing phone out of her purse. She had already decided that whoever it was she would keep them on the line until Detective Patterson lost interest, or maybe she could somehow pretend that it was the landlord calling to say he couldn't meet with her after all.

"Mrs. Blake?" the woman on the other end asked, after she answered.

"Yes," Tamsyn said. She expected it might be some sort of sales call.

"I am calling from the school district. Your son Sean has violated school rules, and is presently at the principal's office. Will you be able to meet him here to discuss further disciplinary actions?"

"What?" Tamsyn said. The words came as such a shock, it took her a few seconds to parse their meaning. "What happened? Is he okay?"

"Yes, *he's* fine," the woman said, and Tamsyn didn't like the way she seemed to emphasize the word *he's*. "We can discuss things further in person. Will you be able to meet him here at the principal's office?"

"Yes," Tamsyn said. "Of course." She looked up and saw Detective Patterson watching her with concern. "I just, it's going to take me a little while. I'm in Scranton right now."

"Very well," the woman on the other end said. She gave some instructions about signing in at the office, but Tamsyn didn't really hear them. She was in a dazed state when the call ended.

"Is everything okay?" Detective Patterson asked.

"Yes, no. I don't know," Tamsyn said. "It's my son. Something happened at school. I have to go there."

"What about picking up your friend's belongings?" he asked.

"I don't have time for that right now," Tamsyn said, and even though her heart felt like it was in her chest, she was grateful for whatever had happened with Sean that saved her from getting caught in her lie about Lisette and her landlord. "I have to go," she said.

She got in her car and started it up. She buckled, pulled out of the parking space and onto the road, and as she drove away she saw Detective Patterson standing on the sidewalk, watching her.

2

Tamsyn could barely comprehend the words the principal was saying to her. Sean was being suspended because according to the principal he had, "inappropriately harassed a female student."

"I'm sorry," Tamsyn said, "but do we know for sure that the girl is telling the truth. This just doesn't sound like Sean at all."

The principal gave Tamsyn a disgusted look. Sean had

not said a word since they had sat down in the principal's office, and Tamsyn felt lost and helpless.

"I'm just saying before we rush to accuse someone, we should make sure we have all the facts straight," Tamsyn said. "You know how kids are."

"Yes, I'm very acquainted with the behavior of teenagers, in particular the behavior of teenagers in my school," Principal Walker said. He was a heavy, middle-aged man whose pale skin tended to turn a bit pink when he became aggravated. It glowed with a pinkish hue as he glared at Tamsyn. "Frankly, Sean's behavior has been troubling for some time, as I explained to your husband during the last incident--"

"The last incident?" Tamsyn interrupted. "What are you talking about?"

"Mom," Sean said. She looked over at him slouched in his chair. He didn't say anything, but made that face he made when he thought she was embarrassing him.

"I'm talking about last month," Principal Walker said. "When it was reported that Sean was bullying another student."

Tamsyn sat there in shock. This was the first she was hearing about this incident. Sean had been bullying another student? She looked at her son, but he made no attempt to deny the accusation. Had he really been picking on another student? Had he harassed some girl?

"Why was I never contacted about this?" Tamsyn asked. "The school had my number. They're supposed to contact me if there's a problem."

"Well, I believe we tried but were unable to reach you. Sean's father is also listed as a parental contact," the principal said.

Tamsyn noticed the way he had deliberately not used

the word "husband" this time around. He must have assumed that she and Ken were separated or divorced, because that would explain why she didn't know anything about the bullying incident. Certainly, it must have seemed unlikely to the principal that such poor communication could exist between two people who lived together.

"So, do you want to explain to me why I'm just learning that you got in trouble for bullying someone?" Tamsyn asked, as they walked across the school's parking lot to her car.

"I thought Dad told you," Sean said.

"Yeah, well he didn't," she said. Of course, it wasn't really fair to snap at Sean about that, when clearly Ken was the one at fault, but that didn't mean Sean was exactly innocent. "Bullying, Sean? What the hell? You know better than that!"

"It's not like that," Sean said. "It was just some stupid thing. It got blown all out of proportion."

"And this?" she asked waving her hand in the air. "Getting suspended? I suppose you're going to tell me this got all blown out of proportion too?"

She heard her mother in her angry words and she cringed a little. Sean seemed to be cringing too, or at least trying to disappear into his hoodie.

Once inside the car, they both sat in silence for a minute or more. Tamsyn took a couple of deep breaths as she tried to sort out the thoughts racing through her head.

"I want to know exactly what happened," Tamsyn said. "Is it true? Were you harassing a girl?"

"It's not like that," Sean said. "She's trash."

The word rang like an alarm in Tamsyn's head. She saw a black plastic trash bag with a severed arm in it.

"Don't say that!" she yelled. Her voice was extra loud in the small space. "We don't call other people trash!"

"Have some chill," Sean said.

"I will not *have some chill*!" she yelled. "You can't go around picking on people."

"It's not like that," Sean said. "I was just trying to help Preston out."

"Who's Preston?" Tamsyn asked.

"A friend of mine," Sean said. "He was dating this girl Lani, but then she started cheating on Preston with his other friend Andrew. So, then Preston wanted me to do him a favor and talk to trashy/not-trashy Lani for him, which is what I was doing, but she flipped out, and that's why I'm getting suspended."

Tamsyn tried to follow the story of the strange and twisted love triangle.

"What did you say to her that she flipped out?" Tamsyn asked.

"That doesn't matter," Sean said. "She's crazy. I was just helping out Preston."

"I don't even know who Preston is. What sort of person is he?" Tamsyn asked.

"Preston's awesome," Sean said. "He's got like this YouTube channel with like twenty thousand followers. He's a cool guy."

"Why couldn't he just talk to Lani himself?" Tamsyn asked.

"Ugh, Mom, it doesn't work like that," Sean said. "I should have known you wouldn't understand."

"I'm trying to understand," she said. "What did you say to her?"

"It was for a video that Preston's making," Sean explained. "He wants to show that she's this total slut."

Tamsyn didn't like the way this was going. Slut seemed like an even worse word than trash.

"What sort of video was this?" Tamsyn asked.

"Does it really matter?" Sean asked.

"I need to know what you did to get yourself suspended," Tamsyn said.

Sean exhaled through his teeth, but instead of saying anything else, he turned away from her and laid his head on the passenger side window.

"This conversation isn't over," Tamsyn said. But a rap on her window proved her wrong. She turned to see Marlena standing outside. She rolled down her window.

"What are you doing here?" Tamsyn asked. She wondered if Philip could have been part of the whole harassment incident, then realized how unlikely it was that perfect Philip was going around harassing a girl for some YouTube video.

"I'm here for that award that Philip's getting from the newspaper. Did I tell you about that?" Marlena asked.

"Yeah," Tamsyn said, and the last thing she wanted to hear about after her son got suspended from school was about how Philip was receiving awards and honors.

"What are you doing here? I thought you were home sick today," Marlena said.

Out of the corner of her eye, Tamsyn saw Sean perk up at this comment. She hadn't told her husband or son about her morning's field trip to Scranton, and when she had left the house had given every indication that she was just leaving for work like she did every other morning.

"I was," Tamsyn said.

"What are you talking about?" Sean asked.

"I was out sick," Tamsyn said, raising her voice in an effort to both drown out and let her son know he should stop contradicting her. "Sean got himself in the middle of some love triangle and is now getting suspended over it."

"Whatever," Sean said. "Do you have any gum in the car?"

"Suspended," Marlena repeated. "Oh my."

Tamsyn felt herself bristling at Marlena's passive aggressive tone.

"It wasn't really his fault," Tamsyn said. She wasn't entirely comfortable with defending her son, when she didn't have all the facts, but she wasn't about to let Marlena get all high and mighty on her.

"You know," Marlena said. "Defending him doesn't really help him."

Tamsyn plastered a too-sweet smile on her face. Beside her, Sean rummaged around looking for gum. She wished she had a piece of gum in her mouth right now, just so that she could spit it in Marlena's face. Not that she would ever do that, but it was nice to imagine it.

She heard Sean open the glove compartment in his search, and too late remembered that it was where she had stashed Jillian's phone. She reached over to shut the glove compartment door, but she wasn't quick enough. Sean held the phone in his hand, the purple glittery case sparkled in the sun.

"What phone is this?" Sean asked.

Tamsyn plucked it out of his hand and shoved it back into the glove compartment, but she wasn't quick enough.

"Isn't that the phone you found?" Marlena said. "I thought you said you turned it in."

"I did," Tamsyn lied. "But the person it belonged to, wasn't able to pick it up, and I was going to drop it off at her house. That's where I was going, when I got the call to come pick Sean up at the school."

The lie sounded less convincing than Sean's excuse that he was getting suspended because he tried to help a friend out by talking to his ex-girlfriend.

"I thought you were home sick," Marlena said.

"Yeah," Tamsyn said. "Look, we've got to go."

Without another word of warning, Tamsyn put the car in gear and peeled out of the parking spot. She drove recklessly through the lot towards the road. Beside her, Sean hadn't buckled his seatbelt and bounced around in his seat.

"What the hell, Mom!" he yelled.

"Sorry," Tamsyn said, as she pulled out onto the road, only slowing down when they were a safe half a mile from the school.

She knew she only had herself to blame for lying to Marlena about that phone, but the whole problem was that Marlena had practically forced her to lie. Marlena had been obsessed with that phone and kept asking her questions about it. It was weird, but then that's how Marlena was, wasn't it? She had been the same way when Tamsyn made the mistake of confiding in her about Ken's infidelities.

Tamsyn regretted losing touch with her friends from school. It happened before she even dropped out. Everything in her life changed after she moved in with Ken, and not necessarily for the better. She couldn't entirely blame the fact that she no longer really saw her friends on Ken. She should have taken a stand. She should have laid down some ground rules for how she spent her time, but she had been stupid and in love.

What it meant was that when she discovered her husband's secret second cell phone six years ago, there was only one female friend she could confide in. As she and Marlena spent their lunch break at Burger King, Tamsyn spilled her guts out to her coworker. There over paper wrappers littered with French fries and drops of ketchup, Tamsyn detailed finding the phone and Ken's reaction.

"Well, you're leaving him," Marlena said. "You have to."

"I contacted that attorney, the one who advertises in the paper," Tamsyn said.

"Good," Marlena said. "I can help you look for an apartment, if you like."

"No, I'm not moving out. I can't afford to, and that's the thing—I don't think I can afford to go through with a divorce either."

"Shut up!" Marlena screamed. The other diners in the restaurant turned to stare. Tamsyn felt herself blush. She glared at Marlena. She had specifically wanted to have lunch somewhere other than the break room, so that they could have some privacy. So much for that.

"There's Sean to think of, too," Tamsyn said.

"Exactly!" Marlena said. Her voice was still too loud, but at least she had toned it down a little. "What do you think being in a messed-up situation like that is going to do to the boy?"

"It's good for him to have a man around," Tamsyn said. She regretted her words almost at once.

"What's that supposed to mean? You think Philip's flawed because his dad ain't around?" Marlena asked.

"No, of course not," Tamsyn said, but even as she said it she found herself thinking about Philip. He was kind of strange. He didn't act anything like Sean or Sean's friends.

Maybe Philip's weirdness came from the fact that he didn't have any father figure at home.

"You can't really be thinking about staying with Ken after what he did to you. He clearly doesn't care about you at all. You need to grow a backbone and make a clean break."

"We've been through a lot, Ken and I," Tamsyn said. "I feel like I owe it to him to at least try."

"You don't owe him shit," Marlena said.

T amsyn didn't exactly feel better after opening up to Marlena, and in the weeks and months that followed she ended up feeling much worse. Marlena didn't agree with her decision to stay with Ken, and she wasted no opportunity to let Tamsyn know this.

First there were the snide little remarks that got under Tamsyn's skin. Marlena would stop by Tamsyn's desk and casually say, "How's life in your loveless marriage?" One day she crushed a cockroach with her shoe in the break room and said that it's a good thing she was there, because Tamsyn would have let the insect move into her desk and would have waited on it hand and foot. Their's was a small office, and the little digs were not lost on their coworkers.

But then there were the other ways that Marlena voiced her displeasure with Tamsyn's decision. She would clip articles out of magazines or self-help columns from the newspaper and leave them in front of Tamsyn's computer. Sometimes she emailed links to articles she found online. Tamsyn tried telling herself that Marlena was just trying in her own way to help. Of course, none of it helped. It only annoyed Tamsyn and drove a wedge between her and her friend.

Marlena used every opportunity she could to point out the fact that Tamsyn had made a grave mistake in not leaving her husband and filing for divorce. The problem was that Marlena had become obsessed with Tamsyn and Ken's marriage troubles.

Even as Tamsyn did her best to put the discovery of Ken's second phone and his cheating behind her and move on with her life, Marlena would bring it up every chance she got. She was determined to not let Tamsyn forget about things.

Marlena's obsession went on for months, until one day Marlena had walked into work with a potted plant in her hand, a violet that she set on Tamsyn's desk.

"What's that for?" Tamsyn asked.

"Peace offering," Marlena said. "I haven't been fair to you. I should have respected your decision to try to work things out with your husband."

Tamsyn was so stunned, she was momentarily speechless. When she found her voice again, she said, "Where's this coming from?"

"Something that happened to me," Marlena said. She waved her hand as if to say whatever this thing was it was completely trivial and inconsequential. "It made me see things in a different light."

"Well, thanks," Tamsyn said, cautiously.

"Still friends?" Marlena asked.

Tamsyn nodded, though she wondered if she and Marlena could ever really be close again. Certainly, she would think twice before ever sharing a secret with Marlena.

And so their friendship continued but was strained, and though Marlena didn't really seem to be obsessed with Tamsyn's marriage anymore, she still couldn't quite resist giving her unsolicited advice and making the occasional dig at Tamsyn's expense.

3

K en hadn't made it home for dinner, and by the time she had a chance to talk with him alone, it was nearly eleven. They were in their bedroom. She protested when he turned on the television.

"I thought you were obsessed with the news lately, what with that dead chick, and all," Ken said.

"Don't joke about that," Tamsyn said, rattled.

"Who's joking?" Ken said. He walked over to the dresser and retrieved the shorts and ratty t-shirt he usually wore to bed.

"We need to talk about Sean," Tamsyn said. "About what happened at school. Something needs to be done about his behavior."

On the television the cop show that was nearly over had reached some dramatic point. Tense music reached a fevered pitch.

"I did talk to Sean," Ken said.

"When?" she asked.

"Before, when you were washing the dishes or whatever," he said. He began to change out of his clothes and into his pajamas. On the television people shot at each other. Tamsyn flinched at each bang.

"What, for five minutes?" Tamsyn asked.

Ken sighed as he pulled the t-shirt on over his head.

"Well, it wasn't a long story," he said. "He told me about what happened at school, and the school administration overreacted."

"The principal said something like this happened before," Tamsyn said. "Why didn't you tell me about that?"

"I did say something to you, I'm sure I did," Ken said. He tossed his dirty clothes in a heap on the floor instead of walking the two extra feet it would take to put them in the hamper. "You know what the problem is? You're so obsessed with that dead chick you don't even pay attention to your own family anymore."

"What?" Tamsyn said. She didn't think that had anything to do with why Sean got suspended, but she couldn't deny the fact that she had taken the day off from work just so that she could drive to the apartment where Jillian had lived. That was crazy and obsessive, wasn't it? Maybe Ken was right. She needed to back off, but even so she couldn't stand the way Ken kept referring to her as the "dead chick." It was unnecessarily cruel and callous.

"Jillian," Tamsyn said. Ken had been about to get into bed, but he froze and turned to stare at her. "Her name was Jillian," she said.

"Like I said, you're obsessed," he said.

"Well, it doesn't have anything to do with why I don't remember you telling me about Sean getting in trouble," she said. "The principal said that happened weeks ago."

On the TV, the end credits began to roll on the cop show and a local news teaser popped up to remind them to stay tuned to find out what the weekend weather forecast held in store.

"It's just proof that you don't even listen to the things I say," Ken said. He got into bed. "Ever since you found that arm with the purple butterfly tattoo on it, you've been acting all weird and obsessed."

At his words, the image of finding the arm in the trash bag flashed into her head, but so did something else, when she had been in the kitchen after she got back from the clean-up and told Ken about her grisly discovery.

"I never told you the tattoo was purple," she said.

"Yeah, you did," he said, but she'd known him long enough to detect the uncertainty in his voice.

"No," she said. "I never did."

"Well, I must have read it in the paper, then," he said.

But she knew this wasn't true, because as Ken said, she was obsessed with Jillian and had read the newspaper stories backwards and forwards. She knew exactly what details were and weren't included in the newspaper accounts.

"It never said anything about the tattoo in the papers," Tamsyn said. She stood rooted to the spot on the bedroom floor, staring down her husband. How well had he known Jillian? Could he have killed her? Had he killed before? Would he kill again?

Ken threw off the covers and got out of bed.

"Well, what other color would a butterfly tattoo be?" he asked, as he grabbed his clothes off the floor and began to put them on over his pajamas.

"Where are you going?" she asked.

"I don't know," he said. "Out. Somewhere I don't have to get interrogated."

He stormed out of the bedroom, and a few seconds later she heard the slam of the side door. She looked out the window and watched as he backed his car down the driveway. Where would he go at this hour? Was there some other woman whose place he would crash at?

The commercial on television was for some sort of medication that had a frighteningly long list of side effects. Tamsyn went over to Ken's night table to find the remote, but before she did, she heard the theme music of the local news and the newscaster said, "Breaking developments today in the Jillian Nelson murder case." Tamsyn spun around to see the TV.

They switched to a video that must have been filmed earlier, because the sun was shining. It showed police entering Jillian's apartment building, and Tamsyn's heart leapt into her throat. Had the news station been filming today while she was there? What if she showed up on the news? How would she explain that to her boss? Forget about her boss. How would she explain that to Ken?

She tried to listen to what the reporter had to say, but it didn't sound like there had really been any developments at all. Her eyes went past the reporter to the cars parked on the street. Was hers there? She was so focused on looking for a silver Elantra, that she almost didn't realize what she was seeing. Wasn't that Marlena's RAV4? The color was the same and that looked just like her proud-parent-of-an-honor-student bumper sticker. Tamsyn squinted at the screen, but they cut back to the newsroom before she could get a better look at it. It had to just be some sort of coincidence. Why would Marlena have been in Scranton?

Unless she was following me, Tamsyn thought.

No, she was being paranoid and ridiculous. Why would Marlena be following her? But it was a little strange how Marlena showed up in the school parking lot right when Tamsyn was trying to leave, and she had been asking all those questions about Tamsyn calling out sick. That was odd.

If there had been any developments in the investigation, Tamsyn missed them. She was too busy playing back the incident in the school parking lot in her head. The news anchor was now talking about a water main break in Hazleton.

What she needed to do was talk to Marlena and find out just what the hell was going on. She picked up her phone but hesitated. This wasn't the kind of conversation to have over the phone. It was time pay Marlena a visit.

She walked past Sean's room and could hear the noises of what sounded like some sort of video game on the other side of the door. She tapped softly, then a little louder when she got no response.

"Yeah," she heard from the other side of the door.

"I need to run a quick errand," she said. "I'll be right back."

He grunted in response.

She started to walk toward the steps, then stopped. Maybe it would make more sense to sit down and talk to Sean. Ken thought the school was overreacting, but what if they weren't? Maybe the person she should be confronting was Sean.

4

Tamsyn's heart raced as she walked up to Marlena's front door. There were lights on in the house, but as she pressed the bell Tamsyn was struck by the realization that it was too late to be showing up like this. Marlena might not open the door. It was a couple of minutes before Tamsyn heard movement inside. She heard footsteps headed to the door, and in a moment it cracked open, the chain still attached.

"Tamsyn?" Marlena said, surprised. She shut the door again, fumbled with the chain, then reopened it wide, waving her coworker inside. "What are you doing here? What's wrong?"

Tamsyn felt suddenly stupid and speechless.

"I just," Tamsyn stammered, "well, I meant. . . I'm sorry."

She turned then, as if she was going to run back out the door, but Marlena put a reassuring hand on her shoulder and guided her gently toward the kitchen. She pulled out a chair for Tamsyn and instructed her to sit as she took out two cups, teabags, a jar of honey and some spoons. Marlena placed teabags in the cups, and Tamsyn watched as she filled them from the hot water tap on her water cooler. Overprotective Marlena had her tap water tested a few years ago and when she found trace amounts of arsenic immediately signed up for a spring water delivery service. She had urged Tamsyn to do the same. Tamsyn had said something about looking into it, though she knew she never would. Her whole paycheck was already spent. She knew she couldn't afford to start having bottles of spring water delivered to her house each month. It made Tamsyn wonder how Marlena was able to afford it all. Sure her house was a little smaller, but how could she afford everything on her measly salary? These were the thoughts running through Tamsyn's head as she watched Marlena stir a spoonful of honey into each mug.

Marlena brought the cups of tea over to the table. She set one in front of Tamsyn, then sat down in the chair on the opposite side of the table. Marlena took a small sip from her cup as she studied Tamsyn, her face etched with a combination of concern and confusion.

"Is everything okay?" Marlena asked.

"Yes—look, I'm sorry for showing up here like this," Tamsyn said. "If I had realized how late it was, I never would have come over."

Marlena dismissed this with a wave of her hand. "We're friends, you can show up here any time of the day or night."

"I know, but really, I'm sorry. I shouldn't have shown up here so late," Tamsyn said. She took a sip of her tea. It was so hot it scalded the roof of her mouth.

"I'm glad you came," Marlena said.

"You are?"

"I've been worried about you," Marlena said. "You haven't been acting like yourself lately."

"Is that why you were following me?" Tamsyn asked. She didn't know she was going to say the words until they were out of her mouth.

"Following you?" Marlena repeated.

"I saw your car on the news," Tamsyn said. "If you weren't following me, what were you doing in Scranton today?"

Marlena looked puzzled, or she looked like she was trying to look puzzled. Tamsyn couldn't help but feeling like Marlena was trying to patronize her somehow. It wasn't anything she could put her finger on, just a general feeling she got. She wondered if this was how paranoia worked.

"I wasn't in Scranton today," Marlena said. "I saw you at the high school, remember? Wait, what were you doing in Scranton?"

Tamsyn ignored the question, and doubled down on her accusation, "I saw your car on the news. You were parked on the street where Jillian lived."

"Jillian?" Marlena said, and there was that puzzled look again. Tamsyn decided it looked too fake to be real.

"The woman who was murdered," Tamsyn said.

She waited for a reaction. Marlena looked at her like she suspected Tamsyn was crazy.

"Wait!" Marlena said, her little shout loud in the small kitchen, "are you sure this picture you saw was from today? We were over there yesterday."

"We who?" Tamsyn asked. It was possible the video could have been filmed yesterday. It definitely hadn't been a live feed.

"Philip and I," Marlena said. "For his YouTube channel. You should see how many views he gets on some of these videos. The one he posted the other day's been watched almost a thousand times."

"But how did he know where she lived?" Tamsyn asked.

"The internet?" Marlena said with a shrug. "He can track down anything. He's a natural-born journalist. How did you find out where she lived?"

"Lisette told me," Tamsyn said.

"The woman you were tutoring? You're not still doing that, are you?" Marlena asked.

"She's come a long way," Tamsyn said.

"I was worried when you called in sick today," Marlena said. "I think finding that dead body really affected you."

"I'm fine," Tamsyn said.

"And then when I saw you at the high school," Marlena said. "When you sped out of there like that, I really didn't know what to think. I'm worried about you."

Tamsyn tried to laugh it all off, but her laugh sounded so fake it frightened her. She took a too-big sip of too-hot tea and sputtered a bit. Marlena stared at her with concern. Tamsyn felt like some specimen being examined by a scientist. In a moment her last wisps of false laughter turned to tears. Marlena tilted her head slightly and waited.

"I haven't been able to stop thinking about her," Tamsyn said after a couple of minutes of near silence. "I can't stop thinking of that trash bag, the way her arm was just sitting there, the wrongness of it."

Marlena reached across the table and stroked Tamsyn's

forearm. Her fingers moved gently over the sleeve of Tamsyn's fleece pullover.

"It's not just that," Tamsyn said. Marlena's quiet compassion seemed to draw the words out of her, or maybe she was desperate to tell someone else, to get out the stuff that she had been keeping bottled up inside her. "That phone I found on the ground? I got a call from it the week before. It was a woman crying. I couldn't really understand what she was saying, but I think she said Ken's name."

At the mention of Ken, Marlena took a break from the concern and compassion to make a little dismissive noise.

"When I finally worked up the nerve to call her back," Tamsyn continued, "and that phone I found was the one that rang, well I guess I freaked out a bit."

"And you think it belongs to the dead woman?" Marlena said.

"Jillian," Tamsyn said. She nodded.

"Oh God, Tam," Marlena said. "You need to go to the police."

"I know," Tamsyn said. Marlena was right, of course. Why hadn't she gone straight to the police with this? "It's going to look suspicious that I waited so long."

Marlena waved this away with her hand. "Tell them what you told me, about Ken."

"I don't know," Tamsyn said.

She stared down into her mostly-full tea mug. Marlena was right about going to the police, but she wondered if it was too late. Detective Patterson had already seen Jillian's phone in her car. Worse than that, she had lied to him about it.

"Listen," Marlena said, clearing her throat. "I'm glad you came over. There's something I need to tell you." She lifted her mug to her lips and finished her cup of tea, but before she said anything else, Philip stepped into the kitchen, his eyes big and wild behind his glasses.

"If you wanted to remove fingerprints from someone's hands you could use a mixture of caustic cleaning products," Philip said.

"Philip, honey, now maybe isn't the best time," Marlena said. "Tamsyn's here. We were just talking about some things."

Philip turned and acknowledged her with a nod, but continued to speak in an excited tone. "I saw a post on Reddit, people were talking about removing their own fingerprints, but then I was thinking that it would work on someone else's hands too. So, that's probably why the killer cut off her hands and kept them."

"Philip," Marlena said.

"That or he could have kept them as a trophy," Philip said. "That happens a lot with serial killers."

He started to talk about serial killers and trophies, but Tamsyn didn't hear him anymore. She stood up with a start, and somehow toppled her still nearly-full mug of tea.

"Oh!" she said.

"It's okay," Marlena said. She gave Philip a warning glare and indicated with her head that he should leave.

"I have to go," Tamsyn said.

"Wait, it's okay," Marlena said. "I'm sorry about that."

But a new surge of adrenaline flooded through Tamsyn, and she ran past Marlena, and back out the front door as Marlena called after her.

~

~

5

When she got home, Tamsyn went immediately to the cabinet under the kitchen sink where she kept all the household cleaners. Just as she remembered, the multi-purpose cleaner bottle was nearly empty when it had been full only a couple of weeks ago. And it was worse than that. She couldn't find a canister of Comet that she always kept there, and a bottle of Pine-Sol that she was sure had been at least half-full was nearly empty. She ran to the upstairs bathroom, the one with the big linen closet where she kept all the bathroom cleaners. The shower cleaner and the toilet bowl cleaners felt suspiciously light, but unlike the multi-purpose cleaner downstairs, she wasn't sure when she had last replaced them.

Did Ken empty out the cleaners in an attempt to remove Jillian's fingerprints? If that was the case, where had he carried out this grim science project? She couldn't help imagining Jillian's severed hands soaking in her bathtub, and even though the shower had been used multiple times since Saturday, she ripped back the curtain only to reveal an empty tub. It was in need of a cleaning, but she didn't see any blood stains.

She spared a glance out the window at the driveway, but there was still no sign of Ken. Probably he wasn't coming home tonight. Where was he? Was he with one of his other women? Did he have a place, some love nest some-where? A little apartment or something? She didn't think he could afford an apartment, even a small one, but then she only had his word on what he was earning. He could have gotten a raise and not told her about it. He may have received more in sales commissions than he let on. Did he have some second home out there that she didn't know about? Were a woman's hands soaking in the tub?

She felt dizzy as she stepped out of the bathroom into the hallway, but noticed the light that seeped out from beneath Sean's bedroom door. She rapped on the door once, and before waiting for a response she opened it. He was at his desk, and he jumped and flipped his laptop closed when she stepped into the room. She wondered what he had been looking at. Porn? That's what kids did on the internet, wasn't it? Well, maybe not all of them. She thought of Philip bursting in to tell them his theory about Jillian's hands.

"Hey, you haven't been doing any cleaning lately, have you?" she asked. Looking around at the state of his room, she knew how unlikely that was, but maybe there was an explanation. "Maybe washing the mud off your bike or something?"

"Um, no," Sean said.

"I seem to be missing some cleaners," she said. "It's okay if you took them, but I was just wondering what happened to them."

"Yeah, I didn't take anything like that," Sean said, and he gave her that look he seemed to give her more and more lately. The one that said, *you're mental*.

She felt like it was her cue to leave, but she sat down on his bed instead. She picked up a fistful of comforter and twisted the fabric through her fingers. She remembered a soft flannel baby blanket, a gift from her aunt after Sean was born. It had been light blue with pale yellow cartoon giraffes on it. She remembered the feel of it in her fingers.

The closed computer on his desk seemed to glare at her. What sort of porn did he watch? Was it innocent stuff or was it dark and disturbing? That was the problem with the internet, it could be such a bleak hellscape at times. She thought of Philip stepping into Marlena's kitchen. Where had he been reading about removing fingerprints with household cleaners? Who were the people posting stuff like this? For a moment the two ideas merged together, and a flash of some sort of imagined porn movie involving severed hands came into her head. She blinked it away quickly, but not before her stomach turned at the idea.

"Philip does some sort of local news vlog thing," Tamsyn said.

"He's a freak," Sean said.

"Don't say that," she said.

"It's true. No one at school likes him."

She sighed, but didn't correct him again. It reminded her of what happened today, getting called into the school, Sean getting suspended.

"Your father said he talked to you about what happened at school," Tamsyn said.

Sean made a movement that was half-shrug, half-nod and all teenager. Had she failed him? Maybe he'd been doomed from the start. Her mother was right. She was too young to have a kid, and look at how badly she had messed things up.

She couldn't help feeling a sense of awe as she looked at her son. How had the little baby she had swaddled in that fleece giraffe blanket seemingly just the other day turned into this young man? It all felt like it had happened in the blink of an eye.

Those first 12 months or so had been rough. Infant Sean had not been good at sleeping through the night. She had to get up multiple times to feed him or just soothe him. She sleepwalked through her days, trying her best to keep up with her schoolwork and go to class. Then there were the chores around the apartment: the never-ending pile of laundry, dishes that needed to be washed, floors to vacuum and bathrooms to scrub. Though Ken had been there, he did not figure in her memory of events. He had slept through the middle-of-the-night feedings. He had not been much help with household chores.

A fleeting memory of one of their arguments from the early days came back to her. She couldn't remember how it had started, but as so many of those arguments from their time in the apartment, it had eventually been reduced to her shouting about not having enough time to do everything she needed to do.

"What do you want me to do?" Ken had asked. "You want me to wash laundry? Is that going to make all the difference?" She realized now he had meant the question as a rhetorical one, as some sort of strange Ken joke, as if the idea of him washing the laundry was the most preposterous idea ever.

"Yes," she had said, taking him at his world. "That would help."

But he didn't wash the laundry. Instead he stormed out of the apartment, slamming the door on the way, and the vibration from the slammed door had done what their shouting had not. It had woken up sleeping Sean. His wails didn't really drown out her anger and frustration so much as they pushed it to the dark, dusty reaches at the back of her head to fester and stew.

"Mom, why do you put up with him?" Sean asked.

The question startled her, and she jumped a little. It was as if he could see straight into her head.

"What?" she asked, returning fully to the present, letting her handful of comforter drop back down to the bed.

"I know he's my father and all, but he's a complete shit-bag," Sean said.

"Don't use that language," she said, almost automatically.

"Well, he is," Sean said. "He doesn't treat you right. I just don't get why you stay with him."

At this his voice cracked a little, and she looked at him with concern. He wasn't crying, but that was only because he was trying so hard not to. His jaw was set in that way that guys did when they were trying to be tough. It made her want to get up and hug him, but she was afraid he would only push her away. So, she sat frozen on the bed.

She told herself she was staying with Ken for Sean's sake. Didn't she put a brave face on and try to pretend like everything was fine? What if that had been worse than the alternative? Sean was not stupid. How long had it taken him to realize that his father was as he termed it, a shitbag? Had he known about Ken's cheating for years? It was yet another mistake she had made. If she had left her husband, it would have been better for Sean, better than growing up in this messed-up home. What sort of example had his parents and their loveless marriage set for him?

They would have been fine together, she and Sean, living on their own. They would have been happy.

"Listen," she said. "I'm going to take a personal day tomorrow. We're going to spend the day together, just the two of us."

"You don't trust me at home?" Sean asked.

"No, it's not that," she said. "We can hang out together. You know, like we used to. We can watch a movie. We'll order pizza."

She felt herself buoyed up with happiness at the thought of a perfect day hanging out with her boy.

"Okay, whatever," Sean said.

Then she did get up and go over to him. She wanted to wrap him up in a tight, smothering hug, but she resisted. Instead, she ran her fingers through his hair, tucked it neatly behind his ears until he jerked away from her and stood up. She let him go, then and walked to the doorway, but she paused there and turned back to look at her nearly all-grown-up boy.

"Hey, don't stay up too late," she said. "We've got a big day ahead of us tomorrow."

THURSDAY

I

FOR THE FIRST time in she couldn't remember how long, Tamsyn woke up feeling happy and excited about the day to come. She had emailed her boss before going to bed to let him know she was planning on taking a personal day. Now she had the whole day to hang out with Sean. It would be the perfect opportunity to reconnect with him. Maybe they should make this a regular event—not him getting suspended, but the two of them just randomly taking a day off to hang out together.

Tamsyn stepped out of the shower and was buoyed to see the day seemed to match her mood. She could see sunlight already streaming in through the bedroom windows. As she dressed, she tidied up the bedroom then made the bed. Ken never returned last night, and he hadn't called or sent any texts either. Had he gone to a hotel room? Maybe he really did have another apartment, or more likely, some woman willing to let him share her bed for the night. She wasn't going to think about any of that. Today was going to be a happy day, and she didn't want to spoil it with thoughts of her husband.

She paused outside Sean's bedroom as she headed down the hall. Behind the closed door, she could hear the sound of his sleep breathing, so much more quiet and pleasant than his father's snores. She would let him sleep. He was a growing boy. He needed his rest.

She went down to the kitchen and took out all the ingredients to make chocolate chip pancakes. Sean had always loved them, but it had been ages since they had made them. With a mug of coffee in front of her, she began to plan out their day. They would definitely watch a movie, but what? Maybe one of the old Disney ones they had watched when Sean was a kid. Ken had always complained about having to watch cartoons, and usually refused to watch the animated movies with them, which meant they were able to enjoy those movies in peace. Yes, they would definitely watch something animated. Then they would order pizza for lunch. What toppings would they get? Well, Tamsyn knew one thing for sure. They weren't going to get onions on it. That was Ken's thing, and even though Tamsyn and Sean hated onions on their pizza, they always seemed to get their pizza with onions on top.

"Just pick them off," was what Ken said.

Today they wouldn't have to pick anything off because they were only going to get the toppings that they wanted. After lunch, maybe they could play a game. She and Sean used to play games together all the time when he was younger. She thought they were still stacked up in the coat closet, but she wasn't sure. Some digging through snow boots and hats might be required to excavate them. Maybe she should do that now, before Sean woke up.

The games seemed to be all the way at the back of the

closet. Tamsyn began to pull out random items and stack them on the ground. Besides the usual Pocono winter gear, there was a light-up reindeer Christmas decoration, a deflated basketball and a taped-up shoebox that was labeled simply "MISC." She had about half the contents of the closet piled up on the floor when her phone rang. It was still sitting on the kitchen table beside her empty mug and she ran back to retrieve it. The number on the screen was local, but she didn't recognize it. Could it be her boss's home number? She was breathless when she answered it just before it could go to voicemail.

"Ms. Blake?" asked the deep male voice on the other end. The voice sounded ominous and familiar. She was silent, as she tried to place it. "Ms. Blake, it's Detective Patterson from the state police."

"Oh," she said, and she let out a breath that she didn't know she was holding. "Has there been news? Have you found out something about Jillian?"

She regretted her words almost immediately. She shouldn't have referred to the dead woman by her first name. It made them sound like they were good friends, and even though a part of Tamsyn felt a kinship with this woman, referring to her by her first name like that was all kinds of wrong.

"As it happens, we have," Detective Patterson said. "In fact, I was hoping you could come down to the station. There were a few things I wanted to talk about with you."

"Of course," she said.

"I can send a car, if you like."

"No, it's fine. I can drive there. I can be there in ten minutes."

More regret filled Tamsyn after the call ended. This would get in the way of the perfect day she had planned with Sean. Well, Sean was still asleep anyway, and Detective Patterson had made it sound like this wouldn't take long. Maybe she could still be back before Sean got up. She jotted a quick note to let him know she had to run out but would be back soon, and that they would order pizza for lunch.

It was only after she got in the car that she thought of Ken. He had never come home last night, he knew Jillian, Tamsyn's cleaning products were missing and now Detective Patterson was calling her and speaking in an ominous sort of tone. What if her fears had been correct? Was Ken a murderer? Had he been arrested?

She drove to the state police station in a daze, her heart racing. If it was true, then her whole life would be upended. But would it?

The more she thought about it, the more she came to realize that her husband being arrested for murder wasn't really that devastating. Yes, there was the horror of the whole situation, of having been married to a murderer, of having likely narrowly escaped being murdered herself, but in other ways it was all sort of a relief. She thought of her plan for her day with Sean. It could be like that all the time, just the two of them hanging out together. They never had to get onions on their pizza ever again.

2

At the state police barracks, she was shown into a windowless room like the one she had been in before, when she initially gave her statement to Detective Patterson. He stepped into the room a few minutes later. His expression was unreadable. He set a manila folder down on the table and sat down in the seat across from her. It was several seconds before he said anything.

"You haven't been completely honest with me, Ms. Blake," he said.

"Mrs.," she said. She wasn't sure why she did. He didn't acknowledge her comment.

"You knew the victim," he said.

"I--" she began, but he held up a hand to stop her.

"Hang on, I'm not done yet," he said. He flipped open his manila folder and looked at the top sheet of paper inside. "We obtained her phone records. She made several calls to you."

"I believe my husband was having an affair with her," Tamsyn explained. "I think maybe my husband had stopped seeing her at that point. But I never met her or knew her name."

"I think it's time we stopped lying," Detective Patterson said, and the look he gave her was so intense that she squirmed in her seat.

"It's the truth," she said.

"Ms. Blake, you showed up at her apartment yesterday. You expect me to believe that you knew where she lived, but you didn't know her name?"

"What I mean is, I didn't know that before," she said. She couldn't bring herself to say the words 'was murdered,' so she just left an awkward pause before continuing. "I only found out her name and where she lived later, the other night."

The detective slid his chair back from the table a few inches. He was silent as he stroked the stubble on his chin. His face looked weary and exhausted.

On the other side of the table, Tamsyn grew increasingly nervous. She thought he had asked her here to answer some questions about Ken, but she was the only one who had mentioned her husband. If she wasn't here because of Ken, then what was she doing here? They couldn't really think she had anything to do with Jillian's death, could they?

But she saw how it looked, her finding the body, then showing up at the apartment. It looked very suspicious, and then there was the phone call. That surely must look like more than some unfortunate coincidence. And as she replayed the last minute or so in her head something jumped out at her.

"Wait!" Tamsyn said. Her voice sounded too loud in the quiet room. "You said several calls? She only called me once."

Detective Patterson sighed. He scooted his chair back up to the table, and began to flip through the papers in his folder.

"Ms. Blake, we have the phone records. You and the victim have been having regular phone conversations for the past four months." His eyes scanned through the paper printouts. "On February 19, you had a call that lasted nearly twenty minutes." He flipped through some more papers before adding, "Here's another call from March that lasted thirty-six minutes."

Tamsyn shook her head. "That's not true," she said. She was confused as she tried to understand what the detective was talking about.

"Ms. Blake, I'm looking at the records right now."

"They're wrong!" Tamsyn said, but her emotions were high and her voice broke as she shouted the words. She hated that it sounded like she was lying.

"Is your phone number not 570-555-8930?" Detective Patterson asked.

Tamsyn frowned. The phone number meant nothing to her. "No, it's not," she said.

"Look, I don't know what to--" he began, but Tamsyn cut him off.

"That's not my phone number. Check your records. You just called me this morning."

This seemed to get his attention, because he paused, and began to flip through the papers to something at the back of the folder, no doubt somewhere where he had her contact details. It was his turn to frown. He flipped back to the front of the folder to take another look at the phone log printouts.

Then he excused himself, grabbed the folder and left the room.

Tamsyn's heart raced as she sat there alone. She tried to reassure herself that this whole thing was some big misunderstanding. It must be some sort of clerical error. Things like that happened all the time at the social security office, but the mistakes could always be fixed. In no time this would all be straightened out, and she could be on her way again.

She thought of Sean at home. He must be up by now. Had he seen her note? Would he be disappointed that she wasn't there? She had her phone with her. She could call, but she knew these rooms all had cameras in them, and she didn't want to do anything else that might look suspicious. So she tried not to fidget too much as she waited for the detective to return.

It must have been ten minutes later when Patterson got back, and this time he was not alone. A younger man with pale, pockmarked skin and smudged wire-rim glasses was with him. He looked as frightened as Tamsyn felt.

"This is Warren," the detective said, indicating the

younger man. "He does our computer research stuff. Go ahead, tell her what you told me."

Warren held a piece of paper in his hands, perhaps one that had come from the detective's folder. He stammered as he spoke. "Um, this phone number, this 555-8930 number, it shows as registered to Tamsyn Blake."

"But that's not true," she said. "I've never seen that number before."

The detective didn't exactly roll his eyes at her, but he tilted his head and looked down at her in such a way that it made it very clear that he thought she was full of shit.

Tamsyn tried to make sense of this new information. Had Jillian somehow registered her phone in Tamsyn's name? Was this some sort of identity theft? She had heard that such things were common, and not all that long ago, she had to cancel a credit card because someone in the United Kingdom had ordered a Domino's pizza with it. It had to be something like that, right? But Detective Patterson had said this was the number Jillian had been calling. So, someone else had the phone number, and then of course, it all made sense.

"It had to be my husband," Tamsyn said. "He must have a second phone."

At this Detective Patterson's eyes lit up. She thought everything was going to be okay. Then he spoke.

"You have a second phone, Ms. Blake," Detective Patterson said.

"No," she said. "Not even a house phone. We cancelled that last year."

"No, you have a second phone. I saw it in your car yesterday," Detective Patterson said.

Tamsyn felt like she had been punched in the gut. She tried to keep her composure. The detective had seen Jillian's phone after helping her open her locked car. She couldn't believe how stupid she had been.

"That phone belongs to my son," Tamsyn said. Would Detective Patterson remember the phone's purple glitter case that didn't exactly scream teenage boy? Probably. Detectives were trained to spot details like that. She tried to work out some story to explain that if he asked. She was leaning towards it being some sort of ironic statement, though she also liked the idea that Sean had lost a bet.

"No more lies!" Detective Patterson roared. Warren flinched at the sudden shout. Detective Patterson shoved his hands in his pockets, and walked to the other side of the room. "How many phones do you have, Ms. Blake?"

"One," she answered. As long as they didn't search her car, she was fine. Why did she still have that phone? Why was she driving around with it in her car? "I really think it has to be my husband. A few years back I found out that he had a second phone, one I didn't know about," Tamsyn explained. "He must have used my name to register his extra phone."

Detective Patterson exhaled loudly before he said, "I've actually gotten a phone before so I'm pretty familiar with how the process works. You can't just put down any name you like. They need identification, they need to verify you are who you say you are. Warren knows that too. Don't you, Warren?"

Detective Patterson turned to Warren, and the younger man looked like a deer caught in the headlights.

"Warren?" the detective repeated.

"Well, actually, sir, sorry," Warren stammered. "I mean, yeah, traditionally they want ID, but if you go to some of those kiosks, like the ones at the mall or something, they don't always check photo IDs and stuff. I mean, I only know because my friend's ex-roommate, once--"

"That's enough, Warren," Patterson said. The younger man stopped talking. He stood there, folding and unfolding the piece of paper he held. "I think you can go now." Warren didn't move at first. The detective waved a hand at him, as if shooing him out the door. "What are you still doing standing there?"

"Oh, I didn't know you meant me, sorry," he said, and he practically sprinted out the door.

Detective Patterson paced around the small room before sitting back down across from Tamsyn.

"You heard him," Tamsyn said. "It would be easy enough for my husband to get a phone in my name. We have a joint credit card."

"Your husband, is he particularly feminine looking?" Patterson asked.

"What?"

"I'm just guessing he doesn't look too much like a Tamsyn."

"It might be different if I was named Karen or Melanie or something, but do you know how many pieces of mail I get addressed to Mr. Blake or that start off 'Dear Sir'? Most people really aren't sure what gender the name Tamsyn is."

The detective didn't say anything to this, but he wasn't silent either. He drummed his fingers on the table, and the sound echoed through the room. Tamsyn couldn't decide what to do with her own hands. She tried folding them on her lap, but then felt weird, and tried moving them back to the table. Nothing felt right.

"Here's what I think," the detective said. "I think it's an awfully big coincidence that a woman who repeatedly called and received calls from a number registered to your name turns up dead, and you're the one to find her body, and then after claiming you've never met this woman or knew her name you suddenly show up at her apartment."

"But that's exactly what it is," Tamsyn said. "A coincidence."

"Where were you on the evening of March 31?" Patterson asked.

Tamsyn counted back days in her head. That was the Tuesday before last. She almost let out a cry of relief.

"I was tutoring. I was at the library," she said.

"Tutoring?" Patterson repeated. "I thought you worked for the social security office."

"I do," she said, "but there's also a woman I tutor once a week. She's learning how to read. We meet at the library. We're usually there 'til around closing, 9 p.m."

"And you go there at what time?"

"We usually meet up at seven."

"So, what you're saying," Detective Patterson said, "is that when I get the security camera footage from the library, I'm going to see you entering the library at seven, and I'm going to see you and this woman in there for two hours until you leave at nine?"

"About nine," Tamsyn said.

"Because here's the thing, if when I review the security camera tapes it doesn't match what you say, it's not going to look very good for you."

Tamsyn tried to remember the previous Tuesday, but it was hard to think. Her mind felt like jelly. All her Tuesday tutoring sessions with Lisette blurred into one. They mostly kept to the same routine, but sometimes one of them needed to leave early, or couldn't make it right on time.

"Wait," Tamsyn said. "That day, I think Lisette had to

leave early. She had a doctor's appointment early the next morning. I think we left at about eight."

"So, which is it? Were you at the library until nine or were you at the library until eight?" Patterson asked. "Because here's the thing if you were only there until around eight I figure that would have given you enough time to have dumped the victim's body at the side of the road."

"It was about eight," Tamsyn said as she remembered the details of the evening. "But I didn't go straight home. I went to Panera. I paid with my phone, there must be a record of that."

"Yeah, but Panera's a take-out place," the detective said. "That doesn't prove anything."

"But I ate there. They must have security cameras too. I was in there a while, an hour or so."

Tamsyn remembered being disappointed that Lisette needed to leave early. She was in no mood to go straight home and deal with Ken. Tuesday nights were her time, her relief from her husband. He wasn't expecting her home anyway. So, she had decided to spend some time relaxing at Panera. She read a book as she nibbled on a pastry and drank her coffee.

"It sounds to me like your alibi keeps changing," the detective said.

"That's not true," Tamsyn said. She tried to remain still and calm as he stared silently at her. His eyes bore into her. She knew she should stop speaking. She had said too much already. What she should do was ask to call a lawyer. That was her right. She thought of the newspaper ad for the divorce lawyer. Did he handle criminal cases as well? He seemed like a nice guy. Maybe she should call him. But wouldn't calling a lawyer make her look guilty?

This whole thing was ridiculous. She wasn't a criminal. How could they believe that? "Look, it doesn't make any sense," Tamsyn said. "If I murdered someone, why would I then go and track down this body I had supposedly hidden and call police about it?"

"Do you know how many criminals can't help returning to the scene of the crime?" Detective Patterson asked. "They have some sick fascination with it."

The words "sick fascination" stuck out for her. She remembered driving home from the police station the day after finding Jillian in the trash bag. Philip had been there at the side of the road. Supposedly he had been there filming something for his YouTube channel, but wasn't it also like Detective Patterson said, he was returning to the scene of the crime? Somehow Philip knew where Jillian had lived and made Marlena drive him there. Then there was last night, that strange gleam in Philip's eye as he stepped into the kitchen talking about Jillian's severed hands, about using household chemicals to burn off the fingerprints. Tamsyn heard Sean saying, "He's a freak." She had scolded him for picking on Philip, but what if Sean was right. What if Philip was some sort of freak?

"Have you interviewed Philip Spinoza?" Tamsyn asked.

"Who?" Detective Patterson asked.

"He's my coworker's son, but he was there that day, at the clean-up, and there's more." So she told him about finding Philip standing at the side of the road watching the police, about him showing up at Jillian's apartment, about what Philip had said last night. "He has a YouTube channel."

~

3

Tamsyn's hands were still shaking when she pulled into the parking lot of the pizzeria. Maybe she needed to eat. She had been in the police station for hours. She turned the car off and pulled out her phone. With her shaking hands, it took her a few extra seconds to select Sean from her favorites. His phone rang, then went to voicemail. Maybe he was in the bathroom or another room. She waited a few seconds before calling again. The voicemail message came on, and she hung up.

She thought about calling back a third time, but then decided a text made more sense. Texts were nice because you could take your time to figure out what to say, and you could look them back over before you sent them to fix anything you didn't like. That's why it took her nearly five minutes to compose and send a text to Sean that in the end said only, *Stopping to grab pizza for lunch. Any requests?*

She sat in the car waiting for his reply. Normally he was pretty good about replying to texts, even if it was just a one-word or emoji reply. Today it felt like it was taking him forever to reply, but when she checked the time on her phone she realized not even a minute had gone by. Her stomach growled. She searched through her purse for a packet of crackers or a granola bar but found nothing. Sometimes she kept stuff in her car. She opened the glove box. There was no food there either, but there was a phone that belonged to a dead woman. She slammed the glove compartment shut.

Tamsyn rested her head against her seat and stared up at the car's ceiling. She needed to get rid of that phone. She was lucky the police hadn't searched her car today, but how long would her luck hold out?

There was a trash can outside the pizzeria. She grabbed the phone out of the glove compartment then grabbed her own purse and stepped out of the car. Her legs felt as shaky as her hands. She stepped over to the trash can and glanced around. There was no one there, but her eyes chanced on something just above her head. A small security camera was mounted under the eaves of the building. She quickly shoved Jillian's phone in her pocket. She would find somewhere else, a trash can that wasn't under surveillance.

They had free sample zeppoles on the counter, and Tamsyn took and ate one as she sat in the booth waiting for her order. She hoped it would stop her shaking hands. Sean had never texted her back. She had ordered a large plain pie for them—at least it didn't have onions. Would he be disappointed that there was no pepperoni or whatever he happened to be craving? Why had he never replied to her text? Was he still sleeping?

Her thoughts turned to Ken. Where had he gone last night? What if he had come back to the house when just Sean was there? She imagined Ken taking Sean somewhere. Where? Maybe he had made Sean go with him and hadn't let him bring his phone. Sean might be in trouble, but no, Ken wouldn't do anything to hurt Sean. That wasn't who he was, was it?

Ken was a horrible human being, and she knew that he was entirely to blame for her becoming the sort of woman who had spent a morning being interrogated by the police. She used to be a different person before Ken. She had promise and potential. Living with Ken had changed all that. If she had listened to Marlena and divorced Ken when she first had her proof that he was a lying, cheating bastard, then she wouldn't be someone the police suspected of being a murderer. She wouldn't be walking around with the dead woman's cell phone in her pocket.

4

The house was quiet when Tamsyn returned. Sean had never replied to her text or her calls. She set the pizza box down on the kitchen counter and headed upstairs to see if he was still asleep. She knocked on his closed door, but there was no answer. When she pushed the unlocked door open she found his room in its usual state of disarray. Sean was nowhere in sight. Her pulse quickened.

She called Sean's and Ken's names as she ran back down the stairs even though she knew the house was deserted. She caught a glimpse of something as she rushed past the living room doorway and froze. Her heart leapt into her throat when she saw a pile of things scattered on the floor. *Someone's ransacked the house*, she thought. A closer look at the pile of random things jogged her memory. It was the stuff she had pulled out of the coat closet earlier when she had been searching for an old board game.

She left the pile of junk and went to the kitchen where she meant to retrieve her phone from her purse, but before she did something on the table caught her eye. It was the note she had left for Sean, but had she really written such a long note? She grabbed it, and saw that appended to the end of her own note was Sean's familiar scrawl.

Went out. See you later. Sean. The big scrawled letters filled the bottom half of the small piece of paper but barely said anything at all. She read them three times. Went out where? Be back when? She didn't have the answers and neither did this useless piece of paper. She crumpled it into a ball and hurled it uselessly in the vague direction of the trash can.

Why would Sean write her a note instead of texting her? But that question she thought she could answer. If he had sent her a text saying he was going out, she would have replied that he needed to stay there. That she would be back soon. The technology may have changed since she was in high school, but the basic premise remained the same: it was easier to beg forgiveness than ask permission.

Another thought crossed her mind briefly. What if Sean had written the note under duress? What if Ken had made him write it before stealing Sean away. Ken wouldn't hurt Sean intentionally, Tamsyn was sure of it, but Ken had always been too reckless around the boy. A fleeting memory of Ken swinging an infant Sean around the living room of their old apartment as if he was a stuffed animal and not a small, fragile human flashed into her head. With her heart in her chest, Tamsyn had snatched the baby away from him, but she wasn't there now to do the snatching, and she didn't know where either of them were. *Probably not together*, she told herself.

The problem with a note scribbled on paper was that there was no way to tell when it had been written. Sean could have written it five minutes after she left to go to the police station, he could have written it five minutes ago, or he could have written it anytime in between. She had no way of knowing.

Maybe he had texted her, and she had missed it. She felt her phone in her pocket and slipped it out. Disorientation swept over her until she realized what she was looking at—not her phone, but Jillian's. She dropped the dreadful object on the kitchen table. She had meant to find some-where to get rid of that thing. It needed to go.

There had to be somewhere she could dump it that wasn't under video surveillance. She could drive over to the Water Gap and take a hike along the Appalachian Trail. Surely there weren't cameras along the Appalachian Trail. She could find some dark, deserted spot in the woods and hide the stupid phone there under a pile of leaves or some-thing. It would work. She was sure it would. She would change into clothes and shoes that were better suited to hiking.

She made it halfway upstairs before she started to have doubts. Even if the trail itself was camera-free, what about the parking lot? They probably had every corner of that lot monitored. It wasn't unreasonable to think that after her morning at the police station the police might be keeping tabs on her, and if on a random Thursday her car pulled into the Appalachian Trail parking lot, and she decided to take a hike, then the state police just might be suspicious enough to send a crew out to search the woods to see if she had possibly left behind any incriminating evidence. There was another problem with this plan of hers. It would mean leaving the house, and she didn't want to miss Sean. He could come home at any time.

No, there was only one solution that made any kind of sense. She needed to physically destroy and dispose of the phone, and she needed to do it in a place that she knew wasn't under video surveillance. Her backyard was a camera-free zone and it was the perfect place to vanish Jillian's phone forever.

Tamsyn usually avoided their garage. It was full of Christmas decorations and boxes of stuff that needed saving for reasons Tamsyn had long forgotten. It was technically a two-car garage, but there wasn't room for one car, let alone two. Somewhere amidst all the piles of crap was a toolbox, and so Tamsyn braved the cold, poorly lit, rank smelling, possibly mouse-infested space to find something to aid her in making Jillian's cell phone cease to exist.

After a solid ten minutes of searching, she finally found the tool box pushed up against the back wall near the far corner of the garage. It took her another couple of minutes to extricate it from the random stack of boxes it was buried under. The stink in the garage grew more intense. She was pretty sure there was at least one dead animal hidden somewhere in this mess. She opened the toolbox lid and was relieved to see a nice, large hammer on top. She grabbed it, opened the garage bay door, sucked in a lungful of cool, fresh air and went out to the backyard. There was a large, semi-flat rock in the backyard. When he had been younger Sean had used it as a make-believe spaceship and a race car. Tamsyn pulled Jillian's phone out of her pocket and positioned it on the rock. The phone was still in its glitter case, and that's what gave her pause.

It reminded her that this object had belonged to someone, a real person, someone who had taken the time to pick out that glittery case, someone who had carried that piece of technology with her everywhere she went, someone who had been cruelly erased from the world. *Someone who slept with your husband*, a little voice in Tamsyn's voice said. No, Tamsyn didn't know that for sure, but if it was the truth, what did she care? If anything, Jillian was more of an ally than an enemy. So, what gave her the right to demolish

Jillian's phone? For all she knew, there was valuable evidence on it that could lead to finding her killer. Maybe she could figure out a way to anonymously turn it into the police. But she couldn't be sure it contained anything about Jillian's murderer. What she knew was that the phone linked her to Jillian, and somehow or other the police would find out that she had been holding onto the thing for days. The phone had to go.

Tamsyn raised the hammer over her head and brought it down on the phone. It made a small, less-than-satisfying mark on the glass face. Tamsyn repositioned the phone so that it was less likely to skitter away and tried again this time putting a little more force into her swing. Her second hit was hard enough to make a noise that echoed in the still air and left the face of the phone scarred with a spiderweb of cracks. She waited a moment, hoping the loud sound didn't attract any nosy neighbors. She didn't hear any signs of movement. She raised the hammer again and delivered a third blow to the front of the phone. The spiderweb of cracks grew and a corner of the plastic case chipped off. She flipped the phone over, and, fueled by adrenaline, she went to town on it. The flimsy case gave way quickly and soon she was digging into the meat of the phone, obliterating the back cover until one of her blows hit the battery and it sprang out of the phone in a smoky explosion. The noxious fumes left her coughing and gasping for air.

She scooped the pieces of phone into a black plastic garbage bag and wrapped it up tightly. She would put it out with the trash tomorrow. As she carried the wrapped bundle back to the garage, she was reminded of finding Jillian in a similar bag. It made her feel ill, but she couldn't think about that now.

She shoved the bag into the trash barrel just inside the

opened bay door. Would that battery start smoking overnight and burn their whole house down? She would wheel the can out to the curb after she put the hammer away, just in case. The dead animal smell hit her as she made her way back towards the corner. They needed to spend a weekend cleaning out this garage, maybe make a whole family day of it.

The hammer didn't want to fit back in the toolbox. She had to keep shifting things around to get the lid to close, but she finally managed it. She needed to rebury the toolbox under the pile of boxes or else Ken would know she had been in there, and he'd have questions. Why hadn't she paid better attention to how the boxes were arranged on top of the toolbox? Her first attempt didn't look right, and she didn't trust it to not topple over. She unstacked them and started from scratch. She took a step back and the topmost box fell off, spilling contents all over the floor. Damn.

She got down on her hands and knees to gather up stuff that should have been thrown out years ago—old drawer pulls, hinges from when they had replaced the front door ten years ago. Why had they saved these things? Something had rolled back into the corner and she had to shove another box aside to get at it.

It took her a moment to understand what she was looking at. Anger rose up in her when she saw the bucket full of dark liquid. Had her husband or her son really been so lazy that they had put some dirty bucket away without emptying it first? Then she realized it was more than just liquid in the bucket. Her first thought was that it was the dead mouse she had been smelling because of that time when she was a kid and she had found a mouse drowned in their backyard rain barrel, but this was no mouse. She realized after a moment that what she was looking at was a hand, a woman's hand.

She staggered backward. She attempted to grab hold of something to brace herself and sent the rest of the boxes that she'd stacked on the toolbox tumbling to the ground.

The garage grew suddenly darker. A shadow blocked what little sun streamed in through the open garage door, and Tamsyn knew she was not alone.

5

Tamsyn spun around. Ken's face was obscured by shadow. Tamsyn grabbed hold of a rake to her left to steady herself and managed to send more boxes toppling to the ground. What had Ken seen? Did he know she had found Jillian's hands?

"What are you doing?" Ken asked.

"Nothing," she said. She tried to sound casual and confident, but she knew she sounded anything but. She needed to be angry with him, not frightened. If she drilled down enough, maybe she could muster up some anger.

"Why aren't you at work?" he asked.

"Why aren't you?" she fired back. There, that was a little better. There was barely a quiver in her voice.

He brushed her question aside as if it wasn't worthy of his response. He took a step toward her, and then another one. Tamsyn had never considered Ken menacing. In all their fights, he had never hit her. He preferred to injure her with his cutting remarks, but now as he approached, she was aware of the nearly six inches he had on her. No one would ever mistake him for athletic, but still he was easily stronger than her. She regretted putting that hammer away.

As he walked toward her she instinctively shied away from him, but she moved in the wrong direction. She should have gone toward the house. Instead she had moved into the far corner, and now she was trapped.

She tried to remind herself that it was just Ken. He was harmless. She had known him forever. But did she really know him? And was he really harmless? She knew the answer to that question. She had seen it in that bucket.

"You've done a very bad thing," Ken said. He stood close enough that she could feel his breath on her cheek. She closed her eyes, preparing herself for a blow that didn't come. Her mind turned to Sean. Would Ken kill her right here in the garage? Would Sean be the one to find her dead body? She would give anything to hold him one last time. To tell him that she loved him. Tears welled up in her eyes. She tried to blink them away and look tough.

"Did you really think you could frame me for murder, you crazy bitch?" Ken continued. Spittle flew from his lips. "You're not some criminal mastermind, Tam. You didn't even finish college."

Fear made it difficult to process what Ken was saying, but she understood the general gist of it. He was trying to confuse her. It was not much different than the lies and half-truths he'd told about his affairs. The goal there was always to make her out to look like some paranoid, over-controlling wife. Now the goal was to convince her that she was a murderer. Did he honestly think she was that stupid?

"They know it wasn't me," she said. "I have an alibi." She hesitated a moment, remembering that her tutoring session had ended early that night and that her Panera alibi was weak. She thought of the camera outside of the pizza place. Surely they must have one inside Panera.

"You're not some criminal mastermind," Ken said again.

"What, and you are?" she asked. She felt defiant now. "You think you're so smart, putting that phone in my name, dumping her body where you knew I would find it during the clean-up. You're the monster."

"What?" he said. He genuinely looked incredulous. She reminded herself that he had years of practice with this lying thing.

He looked like he might have said something else, but then he turned toward the driveway, and she heard it too. Tires screeched and a car roared into view, slamming on the brakes just in time to avoid a collision with Ken's car. Tamsyn's first thought was that it must be one of Sean's friends, but no, she recognized the vehicle: a blue RAV4. She couldn't see it, but she knew that on the back was a proud-parent-of-an-honor-student sticker.

Marlena threw open the driver's side door, and jumped out without turning off the engine. The car chimed to let her know the door was ajar, but she ignored it as she ran into the garage, looking like a woman possessed.

"What the hell were you thinking?" Marlena screamed, her voice hoarse. She stood just behind Ken, her hands planted on her hips as she stared at Tamsyn with fiery eyes. Though it wasn't the reaction Marlena was going for, Tamsyn felt relief. Marlena had rescued her from her homicidal husband.

"You need to call the police," Tamsyn said.

"No, you need to call the police!" Marlena shouted. "You need to call them and tell them you were wrong, you need to take back everything you said about Philip."

Philip. God, Tamsyn had forgotten all about him.

"Those bastards showed up at his school and dragged him down to the police station, because you had the audacity to tell them you thought his vlog was suspicious? What the hell, Tamsyn!"

"Unbelievable," Ken said. "It's not enough that you tried to frame me, you also go and try to frame some innocent kid. You're a psycho."

Tamsyn ignored him. He was trying to bait her and change the subject, but she had seen Jillian's hands in the bucket. She knew what he was capable of.

"I'm sorry," Tamsyn said to Marlena. "I shouldn't have said that about Philip. I was confused. We can straighten that out when the police get here, but you need to call them, okay? Please." She tried to very subtly look in Ken's direction, but she didn't know if Marlena picked up on the cue.

"They're holding my son at the police station!" Marlena yelled. "Do you know what happens to black boys at the police station?"

"Well, well, well, you're as fiery as ever, aren't you?" Ken said, and gave Marlena's arm a friendly pat.

She jerked her arm away.

"Get your hands off me!" she screamed.

"That's not what you used to say," he said with a chuckle. In a mocking voice he said, "Ooh, Ken, you know how to touch me in all the right places."

Tamsyn's confusion turned to shock. She had just found a murdered woman's hands in a bucket in her garage, but somehow finding out that her husband had been cheating on her with her best friend felt like someone had ripped the ground out from beneath her. She saw the way Ken looked at Marlena, and wondered how she had never known about this before. How long had it been going on? They must have both thought she was an idiot. The tears that she had managed to blink away before reappeared, and this time she didn't have the energy to fight them. Instead she took advantage of Marlena's distracting presence to edge past her husband.

She scraped her shins and toppled more boxes in her mad dash, but before anyone could stop her she escaped into the house, slamming the door behind her before locking it.

6

Tamsyn's relief at escaping into the house was short-lived. Yes, the door was locked, but, of course, Ken had a key. How stupid could she be? Why hadn't she run out to her car? But no, she couldn't leave the house. Sean might show up at any second.

She ran to the kitchen and grabbed a chair and wedged it under the handle of the door to the garage. Would that really work? What about the other doors? The windows? She heard movement out in the garage and decided she didn't have time to barricade the rest of the doors or worry about the windows. Instead she ran up the stairs, two at a time, and dashed into the first room she came to, Sean's room. She closed the door and locked it. Her eyes searched the messy room for some sort of barricade, but there was nothing but a lot of dirty clothes and random papers. Sean's desk chair had wheels. It would never work as a barricade. She sat down in the chair and tried to think. What she needed to do was call the police.

She pulled her phone out, but instead of dialing 911, she went to her recents and found Detective Patterson's number. Right now Philip was being questioned by the police. They might even arrest him, and it would be all Tamsyn's fault. Her hand hesitated over the screen. Surely the police were smart enough to know that Philip had nothing to do with Jillian's murder, but she had seen all the cell phone videos of police and young black men. Philip's life might be in danger. Then there was his YouTube channel. The police might leap to the same conclusion she had. She hadn't realized the truth until it was staring her in the face, floating at the top of a bucket in a corner of her garage.

Ken was the murderer, and her life was in danger. Was that why Jillian called her? Was she trying to warn Tamsyn? Tamsyn tried to make sense of her jumbled thoughts. There was no way she would ever be able to explain everything to a 911 operator. She needed to talk to Detective Patterson. The phone rang an impossible number of times, and then the voicemail kicked on. For a second or so she forgot how to speak and then she began to babble. She wasn't sure what all she said. There was stuff about Philip, stuff about Ken. She mentioned something about being trapped and Ken being dangerous and Sean missing, but she wondered if even a trained detective would be able to make sense of her words. She ended the disaster of a call.

She lay her head down on a pile of papers on Sean's desk, but the movement jostled the mouse and woke the computer up. The screen showed a YouTube page. This wasn't the familiar YouTube screen she knew from the funny animal and crazy road rage videos that Marlena was always sharing with her. This was something else. Some sort of backend page. Curious, she navigated through it and saw that it must be Sean's personal account. Like Philip, he must have his own YouTube channel. Maybe all the kids did. She felt hurt that he had never told her about it.

Tamsyn went over to Sean's window. She had a partial view of the driveway from here. Her car was still there, but Ken's and Marlena's looked like they were gone. She pressed her ear to Sean's bedroom door, but she didn't hear anything. Had Ken really left? It could be some sort of trick. She waited in silence, straining to hear a noise from outside the bedroom or out in the driveway. How often did Detective Patterson check his phone messages? He would call her back. He had to. She waited in silence, then curiosity won out and she went back over to Sean's desk and woke the laptop up.

She scanned through the list of uploaded videos. There seemed to be a bunch about some video game. She found one that said something about skateboarding, and hit play. She watched a few seconds of shaky cell phone footage of one of Sean's friends attempting a trick on the steps by the high school. She went back to the list of uploaded videos, and noticed something else, numbers off to the side that showed how many had viewed each video. The skateboarding video had just over a hundred views. The video game ones were all closer to the five hundred mark, but there, up towards the top of the list, were some videos with a staggering number of views. One called "Homeless Prank" had more than two hundred thousand views. She clicked on it.

The filmography was worse than the skateboarding video. She saw Sean's friends outside of a convenience store. One of them had a to-go container of food in his hands. It looked like the sort of thing soup might come in. She heard Sean's voice. He must be the one filming. He said something about dog crap, and the camera jerked to film something on the ground. She couldn't really make out what she was looking at, but she figured it must be the dog crap Sean had been talking about. It was just a stupid video. Boys being gross, but she kept watching. She was fascinated by this secret glimpse into her son's life.

The next part of the video was so blurry and shaky, she couldn't really see what was happening, but she could hear Sean's voice.

"Put it in the stew," Sean said, and then again. "Put it in there. That's perfect, man."

Suddenly the video jumped to a wide view of the convenience store parking lot, and zoomed in on a figure at the far end of it, a homeless man with a sign in the dirt beside him. Tamsyn recognized the man. She had seen him around before, begging for money in different store parking lots. Once or twice she had even stopped to share a few quarters from her purse with him. She remembered the video's title and her stomach lurched. She didn't want to watch anymore, but she couldn't stop now.

Sean's friends came into view and approached the homeless man. They said something to him. One of them handed him the to-go cup. The man took it, and the boys stepped back a few feet. The camera wobbled a little as Sean filmed the man eating a spoonful of the doctored stew.

Sean whispered, "Oh, my God. I don't believe it. He's eating it! He's actually eating it!"

One of the boys let out a little howl, and the man looked up at them, then threw the food container on the ground. The video ended abruptly. Tamsyn felt dizzy and nauseous. She sat there at Sean's desk trying to process what she had just watched. How could this be her son? This wasn't the boy she knew. Where was her sweet, kind son who liked to watch Disney movies with her?

She navigated back to the list of uploaded videos, scanning through the titles. Maybe there was a follow-up video where Sean explained that the video she had watched had been staged, where he explained to his viewers that he and his friends hadn't actually fed a cup of stew laced with dog shit to an unsuspecting homeless man. She didn't see that. What she did see was a video that had nearly three thousand views, but which appeared to have been removed.

However, a thumbnail image remained as did a title, and combined they told her more than she wanted to know. The video showed a teen boy on the ground in distress. It looked like he was crying, but Tamsyn still recognized his face. It was Philip. Then there was the title. It read, *Watch Nerd Get Pranked, Hot Sauce Challenge*. She was glad she couldn't play the video.

She couldn't believe how badly she had failed. How had she been so blind? She didn't know Sean at all. Well, this ended. Right now. She navigated through the page, until she found an option to delete the YouTube channel. She had to tell the computer that yes, she was sure about this, and understood that the action could not be reversed.

She folded the laptop closed and unplugged it from the wall. When she moved it, her hand brushed against a flash drive beside the computer. What was on there? Were there more videos on there?

She reopened the computer and inserted the flash drive. There was only one file on it, a video file. She hit play. This time the camera work was steady, but she realized it was because the camera seemed to be resting on something. She was looking at pine trees and scrubby grass. Someone came into the frame. They were hunched over and dragging something that looked heavy. They straightened up and Tamsyn recognized the back of that hoodie Sean always wore, the one with the illustration of flames on it. The hood was pulled up over his head. He leaned down again and lifted up what he had been dragging. It wasn't a something, but a someone. Tamsyn saw a glimpse of someone's arm pass in front of the camera. A sleeve and what looked like a woman's hand went in and out of focus. Then Tamsyn gasped. For a split second she had caught a glimpse of a familiar tattoo, a purple butterfly. How did she rewind? She wanted to make sure she wasn't making that part up, but before she could find the video controls, someone pounded on the bedroom door.

7

The fist pounding on the door was angry and forceful. Sean! It had to be. She held her breath and waited. The knocking stopped, and she heard footsteps retreat down the hall.

Tamsyn fumbled to try to stop the video with shaking hands. She hit a few random buttons on the keyboard, but the video kept playing.

She didn't want to see a video of her son and his friends murdering a woman. Because she was pretty sure that's what was coming. Unless his friends weren't involved. Unless it was Sean alone who had murdered Jillian.

Why? How? Tamsyn dismissed the questions as irrelevant. If Jillian had somehow tracked down Tamsyn's number, couldn't she just as easily have gotten Sean's number? Had he arranged to meet her? Had he become overcome by emotion and flown into a rage when he found out she was having an affair with his father? Maybe he had never meant to kill her. He could have shoved her and she fell badly. It could have all been some horrible accident. This was still bad, but not as bad as the alternative. She thought of that bucket in the garage, and there was something else nagging at her. There was a noise and movement on the video, Sean's arm and hand came into view and then he moved and she saw nothing but a blurry view of the graphic on the back of his hoodie as his body blocked the lens.

That was it. The camera. It had been deliberately set up to record the scene. Why would somebody set up a camera to record something that was accidental? They wouldn't. This had been planned.

Her son was a murderer. She tried to wrap her head around the idea and found that she couldn't. How had her sweet baby boy grown up to be a murderer? She may not have been a perfect parent. Of course she had made her share of mistakes along the way, but she had always tried her best. She had given Sean nothing but love. It made her think of her mother, and her mother's advice about looking into giving her baby up for adoption.

It might be the best thing you can do for the child.

Would everything have turned out differently if she had just listened to her mother? Would Sean have had the life he was meant to lead and not wound up here? She tried to imagine how differently her life would have been had she followed this course, but her imagination wouldn't go there. She couldn't imagine life without her baby boy. What if it was her selfishness that had led to her son becoming a murderer?

She missed her mother and the conversations they used to have. Her parents were both still alive, but their relationship had changed. She'd had a big fight with them after dropping out of school, and ever since things had been cool and distant between them. Maybe if she had patched things up with them, maybe if Sean had a closer relationship with his grandparents, none of this ever would have happened.

Suddenly the figure in the video moved and Tamsyn could see more than blackness on the screen. Still the lighting wasn't great, and it took her moment to understand what she was looking at. Then she saw Jillian's face partially obscured by the familiar purple glitter phone case. In her other hand she held a piece of paper, and she seemed to be looking at the paper as she typed something into the phone.

Tamsyn heard crying, vaguely familiar crying. Jillian pressed the phone to her face, and all Tamsyn could see in the dim video was a flash as the phone case caught what little light there was. Jillian had called someone, and Tamsyn didn't need to hear the only two words, a tear soaked "No" and a barely audible "Ken" to know who she had called. She felt dizzy.

Sean had given Jillian Tamsyn's phone number and instructed her to call, but why? Had he wanted the woman to apologize to Tamsyn? She needed to speak to Sean. She wished he was here right now. Then the pounding on the door resumed, and she was sure her wish had been granted.

Tamsyn got up and unlocked the door, ready to wrap her arms around her precious baby boy, but he wasn't there.

8

Marlena stood in Sean's doorway. She looked more frazzled than she had in the garage.

"Tamsyn, are you all right?" Marlena asked.

She took a step into the room, and Tamsyn remembered the video was still playing on the computer. Why hadn't she thought to shut the laptop screen? No matter now. She angled her body so that Marlena couldn't really see the video.

"I'm fine," Tamsyn said.

"Ken tried to attack me," Marlena said.

A couple of minutes ago this had been her fear, but even when she had been cornered in the garage by him, her husband hadn't lifted a hand to hurt her. It wasn't his way, and of course he wasn't a murderer. She had made a mistake when she found that bucket. There were three people who lived in this house. She hadn't even considered Sean when she found it.

"Where is he?" Tamsyn asked.

"He ran off," Marlena said. "We need to call the police."

"I already did," Tamsyn said. Would Detective Paterson understand the rambling message she had left?

She thought back to this morning, sitting in that windowless police station room. It had only been hours ago, but it felt like days. She had accused an innocent child of being a murderer when it was her own son who had done that horrible thing, and where was Sean anyway? Could he have gotten scared and run away? No, if he was leaving he would have brought his computer at least. He would be back.

"Listen," Marlena said. "About . . . " Her charm bracelet jingled as she waved her hand in the air. Tamsyn guessed the gesture was supposed to indicate her affair with Ken.

"We can discuss this some other time," Tamsyn said.

"I always meant to tell you about it," Marlena said. "It's just, well, I thought I would wait until after you were divorced. It was cowardly of me, I know, but I figured--"

A scream interrupted Marlena. Even coming through the laptop's built in speaker it was loud and blood-curdling.

"What was that?" Marlena asked.

"Just some movie. Netflix or something," Tamsyn said nodding towards Sean's computer.

"You were in here watching a movie?" Marlena asked.

"Sean must have left it running," Tamsyn lied.

She reached back to shut the laptop before Marlena could see anymore, but her hand froze before it lowered the lid. The sleeve of Sean's hoodie pulled back half an inch to reveal something that shouldn't have been there. Like the glimpse of Jillian's butterfly tattoo earlier this was just the briefest flash of something. She couldn't even be sure that she had seen it. Could her desperate mind be playing tricks on her? The video was so dark and grainy how could she have possibly seen a small Pandora bead?

She closed the lid and turned around. Her eyes went immediately to Marlena's wrist where the familiar bracelet was. Had she really just seen that in the video? She looked up into eyes that looked cold and murderous and knew that it had been no trick.

Thoughts raced through her head. Sean wasn't a murderer. Marlena was. Sean was missing.

"Where is he?" Tamsyn demanded. "Where's Sean?"

"How should I know where that worthless son of yours is?" Marlena asked.

"What did you do to him?" Tamsyn asked.

"What did *I* do to *him*?" Marlena spat. "He deserves to rot in jail for what he did to Philip. Your son is trash, just like his mother."

"Where is he?" Tamsyn repeated and she lunged at Marlena and grabbed her shirt, but the bigger woman easily pushed her away.

"You make me sick," Marlena said. "He didn't love you, you know that? He told me that, but still you stuck by him like the pathetic creature you are."

For a moment, Tamsyn was confused, but then she realized that Marlena wasn't talking about Sean. She meant Ken. Tamsyn agreed with everything Marlena said.

She didn't deserve Ken. She deserved someone so much better.

"I should have divorced him," Tamsyn agreed. She needed to placate Marlena, calm her down so that she could find out where she had taken Sean.

"You should have, but you're a selfish bitch, aren't you?" Marlena said. "We had plans, you know. We were going to buy a little house down by the shore. We were going to start fresh, but no, you had to go and screw everything up. Do you know what that was like for me, every day having to hear about Ken-this and Ken-that and your perfect family?"

"He could have filed for divorce," Tamsyn said, "if he wanted to." They weren't placating words, and she regretted them.

"And he would have, but then you two had your heart-to-heart and you convinced him that he should stick around and try to work things out," Marlena said.

Tamsyn tried to recall the conversation that Marlena was referring to. A heart to heart with Ken? Talking about working things out? She couldn't remember anything like that. Moreover, she knew she had never told Marlena she and Ken had any conversation like that. It must have been a lie that Ken had fed Marlena, probably when she was begging him to leave Tamsyn and Sean and start a new life with her.

"You never gave him an ounce of respect," Marlena continued. "You pushed him away, pushed him right into the arms of all those stupid, worthless women. Do you have any idea what that did to me?"

"You followed him around?" Tamsyn asked as the realization slowly came to her.

"I had to," Marlena said. "He shut me out. I had no other

choice. I'm the only one that really cares about him, not you, not those other whores."

"Jillian," Tamsyn said.

"She was the worst of all, complete trash. She started stalking him. She wouldn't leave him alone."

Just like you, Tamsyn thought, but didn't say. She couldn't believe that so many women could be fighting over her worthless husband, but then she too had stayed with him, against all reason.

"On the phone you can be anyone," Marlena said. "So, I was you. It was easy to pretend I was some weak, spineless creature."

"The second phone," Tamsyn said remembering Warren's explanation about how some cell phone kiosks didn't check ID very carefully. "How could you afford it?"

"You know, I almost feel sorry for you being so stupid," Marlena said.

"Ken gave you the money?" Tamsyn asked.

"Ken didn't give me shit. I worked for every penny I made," Marlena said. "You know how many desperate people walk through the doors of the social security office? It's only idiots like you who go around tutoring them for free. I charge good money for filling out their applications so that I know they'll get approved, then I get ten percent of their monthly check."

"They pay you?" Tamsyn asked.

"They have to, don't they? Otherwise I'm going to report them for fraud and they won't be getting any money from Uncle Sam."

The revelation made Tamsyn's head reel. How long had this been going on? How had Marlena gotten away with it? But, of course, Marlena knew the system better than anyone.

"So you pretended to be me on the phone so that Jillian would leave Ken alone?" Tamsyn asked.

"Somebody needed to set her straight," Marlena said.

Tamsyn thought of that trash bag where she had found Jillian's remains. She had been unable to imagine the monster who would do something like that, and never in a million years would have guessed that it was her friend and coworker.

"But, Marlena, why?" Tamsyn asked.

"Bitch got too nosy," Marlena said. If Tamsyn wasn't afraid for her life, she might have laughed at the irony. "She found out who I really was, and that psycho said she was going to report me to the police. Not on my watch."

Of course, it was Marlena who was truly the psycho one. Tamsyn couldn't believe she had been so blind. Her sense of self-preservation began to kick in. She was alone with a murderer, and that murderer had just made a full confession to her. She needed to get out of here.

"Why are you telling me this?" Tamsyn asked. "Aren't you afraid I'll tell the police?"

"Ha, like what you tell them has any value," Marlena said. "We already know you would say anything to save your own neck, like trying to pin a murder on an honor student, for God's sakes. And when your son is arrested for murder, when the police find a *video* of him murdering that woman? Well, naturally, you make up some ridiculous story about your coworker to try and save him. Don't you remember that old story about the boy who cried wolf? No one's going to believe a word you say."

Marlena was right. The evidence did alarmingly point to Sean. Jillian's hands in that bucket in the garage, Sean's hoodie in the video, the flash drive in his room. And, she reminded herself, if the cops were to search her trash can right now, they would find the smashed up remains of Jillian's cell phone. Of course, if the police really examined that video, they would see what she had seen, wouldn't they? She needed to tell them what to look for. Uncertainty welled up inside her. Had she really seen Marlena's bracelet in the video? Had it been a cruel trick of the light?

"Did you break into the house to plant the evidence?" Tamsyn asked. She was curious, but also stalling for time.

"Why would I break in?" Marlena asked. "I just used the copy of your house key that I made one day on my lunch break."

"I don't know who you are," Tamsyn said.

"I'm the woman you cheated out of a life of happiness," Marlena said.

Tamsyn debated whether or not she should tell Marlena that more likely she had saved her from a life of misery with Ken, but before she made a decision she heard someone run up the stairs.

9

Tamsyn looked past Marlena to see Sean in the hallway. She tried to silently signal to him to be quiet without alerting Marlena to his presence but failed.

"What the hell?" Sean said.

Marlena spun around at the sound of his voice.

"Go," Tamsyn said. She tried to shout the word but her voice was too weak. "Call the police."

Marlena looked between Sean and Tamsyn.

"I thought you already did," Marlena said to Tamsyn. There was a glint of a smile in her face, like she had caught Tamsyn in a lie.

"Mom? What's going on?" Sean asked. He still stood in the hallway. He hadn't followed Tamsyn's instructions. "Why are you in my room?"

Tamsyn saw his eyes flick to the computer.

"Just go," Tamsyn said again, her voice so weak it was practically a whisper.

"I have a better idea, Sean," Marlena said. "I think you should come in here and join your mother." Then like some gracious host, Marlena waved her arm to indicate his room. Even though Tamsyn frantically shook her head, Sean followed Marlena's instructions.

He went to his mother and whispered urgently to her, "Were you on my computer?"

"Why don't you both have a seat on the bed?" Marlena said in a fake, sickly sweet voice.

"Marlena, this is between you and me. Leave Sean out of it," Tamsyn pleaded.

"Oh, that's where you're wrong," Marlena said. "Your whole screwed-up family is part of this. You know what you are? You're a family of bullies. You're a bully and Ken's a bully and, what a surprise, you raised a nasty little bully son."

"Screw you," Sean said, he turned around to give Marlena a dirty look.

"Sean, please," Tamsyn said, but he continued to stare defiantly at Marlena.

"Save your breath, Tam," Marlena said. "You're a bit lacking in the whole parenting skills department, don't you think? I mean, the proof is staring you in the face." She nodded at Sean.

Sean ignored both of them. He grabbed a backpack off the ground, and began to shove random articles of clothing into it.

"Whatever," Sean said. "I'm going over to Preston's."

He went to grab the laptop off his desk, but Marlena grabbed hold of his arm.

"That stays here," she said.

"Fuck off," Sean said. "You're not the boss of me."

"Watch your mouth, young man," Marlena said, and she shoved him away from his desk in the direction of the bed. Her shove was strong and caught him off guard. He stumbled, but didn't fall. He whipped around like he might try to fight back but froze.

Tamsyn was briefly proud that he was too well-bred to hit a woman and simultaneously annoyed that he would pick this moment to learn some manners, but she was mistaken about the cause of his sudden hesitancy.

"That's the bracelet!" Sean yelled. He stared at Marlena's wrist as if a deadly viper were coiled around it. So it hadn't been a trick of the light, after all.

"Sean, don't," Tamsyn said, but he was too excited by his realization to listen.

"That was the bracelet in the video," Sean said. "You were the one wearing my hoodie! You murdered that woman!"

"What?" Marlena said. She looked shocked.

Tamsyn remembered Ken telling her she wasn't a criminal mastermind. Clearly, Marlena wasn't either despite her social security scam. Marlena hadn't seen her bracelet in that video, but if she and Sean both had then the police would as well. That was, if they got a chance to watch the video.

Tamsyn lunged past Sean and yanked the flash drive out of the computer. Marlena grabbed hold of her. She clawed at Tamsyn's arm, but Tamsyn kept the flash drive clutched in her fist.

"Mom!" Sean screamed.

"Go get someone," Tamsyn told him. Marlena yanked her hair and scrabbled to get at the flash drive, but Tamsyn refused to give it up. "Go!" she screamed again at Sean, and finally her son listened.

He ran toward the hall. Suddenly Marlena let go of Tamsyn. It all happened so quickly Tamsyn barely realized what was happening. Marlena told Sean to freeze, and the next thing Tamsyn knew her coworker had a gun in her hand and was pointing it at her son. It was an ugly, black handgun. Tamsyn watched in horror as Marlena's finger began to squeeze the trigger. She dropped the flash drive. She ran full speed at her son, determined to get him out of the way of the bullet.

The boom of the gunshot deafened Tamsyn as she and Sean toppled to the ground. It was all she could hear as she lay on top of him. Frantically she began to check him for a wound. Sean pushed her away. That was good. He still had some fight in him, but she needed to stop the bleeding. He said something to her, at least his lips were moving, but all she could hear was the echo of the gun.

Then someone ran past them into the bedroom. Another person followed. Cops, she realized as she stared at their uniform pants. One of the cops squatted down to where she and Sean were. The officer said something to them, but Tamsyn's ears still weren't working. She shook her head. The police officer helped Tamsyn to her feet, and as she moved she saw blood. *Sean!*

She made another effort to find his injury, but Sean pushed her away. He wasn't hurt. She looked at the ground, at the blood. It wasn't Sean's. Marlena lay on the ground. Blood pooled around her arm, the one that had held the gun. The gun lay inert on the ground, inches from her wrist, with its sparkly Pandora charm bracelet.

Police officers surrounded her. The officer who had helped Sean and Tamsyn to their feet now ushered them out into the hall and out of the way of the paramedics, who rushed in with a stretcher. Her ears still rang as she watched the chaotic scene unfold in the bedroom, and tried to piece everything together.

Marlena never fired her gun. The police showed up just in time to stop her. They must have already been in the hall when she had tackled Sean. Her stomach twisted as she thought how close they had come to being killed. She could have just as easily pushed Sean into the path of the officer's bullet when she was trying to save him.

"Mom! Mom!"

Tamsyn's ears still rang, but she could hear Sean. It sounded like he was far away and not right next to her, but she could hear him.

"Are you okay?" he asked. She nodded, and she wrapped her arms around him and hugged him tightly to her as tears began to roll down her face.

She blinked them back, and looked up to see Detective Patterson walking up the stairs toward them. She loosened her grip on Sean, but she wasn't ready to let go of him entirely.

"I got your message," Detective Patterson said, as he nodded towards the mess in Sean's bedroom.

"I'm surprised you could understand it," she said.

"To tell you the truth, I didn't, but I figured it might be a good idea to send some officers over to check things out."

The paramedics had Marlena strapped to a stretcher. They held an oxygen mask to her face as they wheeled her out of the room. Tamsyn saw the bracelet still on her wrist as they wheeled her past.

"There's a flash drive on the floor in there," Tamsyn said to Detective Patterson. "It has a video on it. I think it will help with your investigation."

SIX MONTHS LATER

TAMSYN LUGGED the last of the boxes into the small galley kitchen off of the apartment's living room. She looked at the small number of cabinets and the large number of boxes and wondered if she would be able to make it all fit.

"That looks like it's the last of it," her mom said. Tamsyn smiled at her mother, who was standing in the doorway. She was reminded of the last time her mother had helped her move into an apartment. There had been less gray in Mom's hair then, less wrinkles on her face, but she had been the same take-charge person. For a moment she felt a pang of sadness thinking about all the years they had lost, all those years when they had barely spoken to each other.

After Marlena's arrest, after Tamsyn had decided to finally file for divorce, she knew it was time to have a real conversation with her mother. Picking up the phone and making that call hadn't been easy, but she was so glad that she had done it.

She had been considering changing jobs and returning to school to finally get that degree. So, she turned to her mother for advice. She had regrets about not listening to her mother in the past, but this time around she noticed something about her mother's counsel. Nothing her mother said seemed very definitive.

"What matters is what you want," her mother said that afternoon as she sipped her coffee on the patio outside Panera. "If returning to school and getting a teaching degree is what would make you happy, you should do it."

"That's a big change from the kind of advice you gave me when I was in college," Tamsyn observed.

"Is it? Well, the general idea hasn't changed at all. All I ever wanted was for you to be happy," her mother said.

"If I had listened to you, Sean would be so much better off," Tamsyn said, and she tried to imagine the idyllic life he would have had with whatever couple had adopted him.

"He seems to be doing pretty well, if you ask me," her mother said. "He's got a mother who loves him."

Tamsyn had one of those too, and she regretted that it had taken such an ugly series of events to make her realize that.

Now, as she stood in her new apartment's too-small kitchen, surrounded by boxes, she understood that love had been there all along. She had been the fool who'd tried to shut it out.

Her father poked his head through the kitchen doorway, and said, "It's after three. If I get the truck back before four, I won't have to pay a penalty."

"It's after three?" Tamsyn asked. She had lost all track of time. Visiting hours ended at five. If she followed her parents to drop off the truck, then drove them back to the house to pick up their car, that wouldn't leave her enough time.

"Would you mind coming with me to visit Sean after we drop off the truck?" Tamsyn asked. She noticed the look her parents exchanged and hastened to add, "You wouldn't have to come in with me. You could wait in the car."

"Honey, we'd love to visit Sean," her mother said.

The police had confiscated Sean's computer as well as the flash drive, and so along with Marlena's video they saw the others, more even than she had watched. It was enough for them to charge Sean and his friends with crimes. His friends had better attorneys and had gotten off with community service. She had seen one of them last week shelving books at the library. Sean was serving six months at the juvenile detention facility.

Though she had cried when she learned about his sentence, she had come to see his punishment as a good thing. It was good for him to learn that his actions had consequences, and maybe she was being naive, but she felt like this was the wake-up call that he needed. The new facility with its sleek and modern design and its more compassionate approach felt more like a boarding school to Tamsyn than a jail.

Lisette was there to check them in when they arrived. She kept an eye on Sean when she was working, and texted Tamsyn with her newly purchased phone on her work days. That, coupled with Tamsyn's daily phone calls with Sean, made her feel like she knew more about her son than she had when they were living together.

"Nice place," her dad said as they stepped into the visitors' lounge.

Sean was surprised but happy to see his grandparents there.

"Grandma and Grandpa were helping me move into the new apartment," Tamsyn explained when they all sat down at one of the tables. "It does have two bedrooms, but it's small, so you'll probably want to stay with your father at the house when you're ready to go home."

"No way," Sean said. "Why would I want to live with him?"

And it made Tamsyn wonder why she had lived with Ken for so many years. Filing for divorce had changed things for her. She felt like it was the first step in getting her life back. For the first time in a long time, she felt truly happy. She thought of what her mother said. It was true. All she wanted for Sean was for him to be happy. She had done him no favors staying with Ken. Being around someone who treated people the way Ken did hadn't been healthy for either of them.

Maybe that was what drove Marlena to madness, to do the horrible thing that she did. Tamsyn wasn't sure she would ever understand the actions of the woman she had once considered a friend, but she knew that someday soon the still-fresh image of that terrifying afternoon in Sean's bedroom would fade. Maybe in another six months, maybe in a year, but soon there would come a time when she didn't experience daily flashbacks to Marlena pointing that gun at Sean, to those chaotic, silent moments after a police officer's bullet had disabled the would-be assailant. How long would it be before the whole ugly mess became nothing more than a distant memory?

∾

PLEASE REVIEW THIS BOOK

I know you're busy, but it would mean a lot to me if you could take a few minutes out of your day to write a review of this book. Reviews help authors by improving search rankings and letting other readers know if this is a book they would enjoy reading.

I am eternally grateful to readers who take the time to leave reviews on the sites of the retailers where they've purchased my books.

ALSO BY ALISSA GROSSO

For Adults

Girl Most Likely to Succeed

For Young Adults

Unnamed Roads

Shallow Pond

Ferocity Summer

Popular

Non-Fiction

How to Make Money Selling Vintage Items on Etsy

ABOUT THE AUTHOR

Alissa is the author of seven books. She lives in Pennsylvania and when she's not busy writing or selling stuff on the internet she's probably hanging out with her boyfriend Ron or walking her dog, Jack. She shares her writing adventures on her weekly Awkward Author vlog and podcast.

For more information visit:

alissagrosso.com